MURDER WORE A MASK

MYDWORTH MYSTERIES #4

Neil Richards • Matthew Costello

RED DOG
UK

Published by RED DOG PRESS 2020

Originally published as an eBook edition by Bastei Lübbe AG, Cologne, Germany, 2019.

Edited by Eleanor Abraham
Cover Design by Oliver Smyth

ISBN 978-1-913331-13-9

www.reddogpress.co.uk

MURDER WORE A MASK

1.

PARTY TIME

HARRY STOOD AT THE bay window of the Dower House's compact sitting room, looking out at the garden in the early evening light.

The gardener, Mr Grayer, borrowed from his Aunt Lavinia, had done an artful job of trimming the hydrangea, and getting all the other bushes and shrubs into an orderly array.

While Harry himself enjoyed messing about in the garden, he and Kat had been so busy, to-ing and fro-ing from Mydworth to their flat in London, it was best to leave the gardening in the capable hands of a professional.

He was tempted – standing by the window, in full fancy dress – to pour himself a few fingers of scotch.

Tonight was going to be one long evening. A big party at Mydworth Manor – the type of party that he thought only his Aunt Lavinia could pull off.

A full-on Venetian masked ball, guests by the hundred, champagne probably on tap the whole night.

Pacing oneself was a good course of action.

He stood there, waiting for Kat to appear, curious what her chosen costume – hidden until tonight – would be.

He heard the sound of steps on the nearby staircase leading down from the upstairs rooms.

He turned to see Maggie, their housekeeper – and the person Harry had known longest in his life – as she came into the room, broad smile on her face.

"You all set, Sir Harry?"

"Now don't you scare me, Maggie. Will I be able to recognise my—"

Then, only steps behind, her black carnival mask already on, dark hair pulled back, he saw Kat.

That is my wife in that absolutely stupendous outfit.

"Well, well, well." Without a word, Kat glided over to his side. "I do believe you have me speechless, Lady Mortimer."

"Like it?"

"Love it."

The long velvet dress – with a low-cut bodice, hugging her frame tight till it spread to a V that went to the floor – fit perfectly. No doubt helped by a stitch here and there by Maggie.

And the shimmering black material seemed to absorb all the light – and then some – in the room.

"You look," he searched for the *mot juste*, "absolutely stunning. But who are you supposed to be? Not that I mind, because whoever it is, well… wow."

Kat laughed. "Your aunt sent over some wonderful designs weeks ago. Picked this one. It's called 'courtesan'."

"Is it? Remind me now, what exactly do courtesans do?"

Kat gave a little twirl, obviously enjoying the effect her outfit was having on him.

"Well who knows, Sir Harry. I imagine we will find out tonight."

Harry turned to their housekeeper. "And I suppose you helped this along, eh, Maggie? I do believe you missed your calling."

Maggie grinned broadly. "You better be ready for a lot of eyes taking the two of you in!"

"So, Harry," Kat said, "any clue for me who *you're* supposed to be?"

Harry's outfit nearly matched Kat's in sumptuous material, but the comparison ended there: a waist-length cape, open to show a ruffled white shirt, unbuttoned at the top; trousers that fit more like dancer's leggings; and all of it topped with a cap that he could only describe as "rakish", complete with an iridescent feather shooting out the back.

"I'd better just tell you. I… am a pirate."

Harry grinned as he stuck one leg out, and did a half bow.

"I've met some pirates in my time, but that…"

"Not *exactly* what I expected either. But apparently, back in the days of Walter Raleigh, and other sea-faring rapscallions, the commanders of ships that did the looting also had a keen sartorial sense."

"And that?" said Kat, nodding to the cutlass that swung from a belt around his waist.

Harry stepped back a safe distance, and, with a swish of steel, drew the long blade and adopted a duelling pose.

"Courtesy of great-great-uncle William, renowned swordsman of the 16th The Queen's Lancers, and hero of the Battle of Aliwal back in '46, don't you know!"

He carved the historic sabre through the air a few times, as if parrying unseen attackers, then returned it to its scabbard.

"Normally lives in the ballroom up at the manor. Lavinia said I can hang onto it. Thought I might stick it on my study wall."

"Well – I know who to come to if my honour needs defending," said Kat.

"Don't count on it," said Harry. "Last time I had a sword fight I was at school."

"You know, Harry, that's not something you hear people say much back home in Brooklyn."

"Fencing! Good God, woman! All part of an English gentleman's education."

She took a step closer to him. "You have not forgotten a *mask*, have you?"

Harry reached into a side pocket on the inside of the cape, pulled out a bright red mask, and slid it on.

And for a moment he stood there, looking at his suddenly serious wife while she gazed at him, the masks working their magic.

Thinking… *maybe let's just forget about the party.*

"Time you two were going. I'll do any clearing up. Things will be nice and tidy whatever hour you get back here."

Harry turned to Maggie. "Sure you won't come too? I'm sure we could whip up something quick that would suit you?"

Maggie laughed. "My days of fancy-dress parties ended *long* ago, Sir Harry. To be honest, I don't think they ever started. Now, hurry along. Who knows what support your dear aunt may need!"

Harry took Kat's hand, and, as if escorting some beautiful stranger, he walked her to the door.

A "night in Venice" was about to begin.

FEELING A MILLION DOLLARS in her amazing dress, Kat walked arm in arm with Harry, down the long drive towards Mydworth

Manor, flaming torches every fifty yards or so, making the event seem more like a medieval pageant.

In the distance, across the gentle slope of the meadows, she could see the manor house, glowing in the golden light of the early evening. The sounds of a jazz band drifted towards them, mingled with distant laughter and conversation.

It seemed the party was in full swing!

Every now and then a vehicle rolled past filled with masked guests in ever more exotic outfits – cardinals, soldiers, dancers, jesters, French courtiers – all crammed into open-top cars, laughing gaily.

Something surreal about it all, she thought.

Other couples coming from the town had clearly also decided to walk, not drive. And Kat thought she recognised some faces behind the masks – and also new friends she had made since arriving here as Harry's mysterious New York bride.

"Tell you one thing, Harry. Your aunt sure knows how to throw a party," said Kat.

"Oh yes. When I was growing up here, they were a regular event," said Harry. "And you never quite know who you're going to meet."

"The great and the good?"

"And the bad too, sometimes. Lavinia has quite, um, broad tastes. Long as you're fun and interesting, that's all you have to be to get an invite. Though, of course, there are always those who are invited because they have to be."

"Can't wait to meet them – good and bad, and in between," said Kat, as they reached the house and joined a small throng of guests climbing the great steps towards the already packed entrance hall.

At the door she was greeted with a glass of champagne from a footman, and she stepped through, already thrilled by the party atmosphere.

At her side, she saw Harry shaking hands in every direction. He grabbed her hand – a great feeling amid this sea of people – and they forced a path through the crowd towards the living rooms.

"Let's go find the music, shall we?" he said, and off they went. "The night is young. And, it turns out, so are we…"

2.

A NIGHT TO REMEMBER

KAT HAD BEEN TO many grand parties in her time working for
the American government, in various capital cities across Europe.

But this one? Something else entirely.

All the Manor's ground-floor rooms had been thrown open –
even the Grand Ballroom at the back of the house, which was
rarely used: so far she'd only ever seen it covered in dusty white
sheets with shutters closed.

Now she could see that the great room positively sparkled,
mirrors dazzling, chandeliers bright, the intricate parquet floor
spotless as a crowd of guests swayed to the music of a four-piece
jazz band that played in the corner.

Not dancing yet, she thought, but, at the rate the champagne was
flowing, it clearly wouldn't take long.

Harry led her through other rooms, all just as packed. He gave
her a running commentary as they slipped, hand-in-hand, through
the crowds and past long lines of buffet tables at which masked
guests queued for food.

"All right. See the lady by the fireplace in ostrich feathers?
Caused rather a scandal with the prince, last year."

"Don't need to guess *which* prince," said Kat.

"The Royals – always entertaining. And those chaps having a chinwag in the corner…" Kat looked across to where a group of elderly men in Arabian robes stood smoking cigars. "Some of our most illustrious generals, I do believe. Fella on the chaise longue in the cowboy outfit – American novelist, very popular. What's his name, always forget. Oh look – out on the terrace there…"

Through the open French windows Kat caught a glimpse of a tight cluster of men and women in vivid colours, all shimmering Chinese silks and elaborate Indian headgear.

"Lavinia's old Bloomsbury pals. Painters, writers, theatre directors, what have you. Hard to tell if they're in fancy dress or not. Wonder who'll be sleeping with whom by the end of the evening? We should run a lottery! Oh… and look."

Kat followed his subtle nod to the door.

"Rare sighting of the Leader of the Opposition. Dressed as Robin Hood. Good lord, look at those tights. Too tight, to be sure."

Kat laughed, then pointed to a pair of bishops in purple leaning against the door chatting earnestly.

"Those two?" she said.

"Actually," said Harry, "they're real bishops."

"Gosh, I'll have to mind my language."

"Oh, don't bother – off duty you wouldn't believe the stories I've heard them tell."

Kat heard some cheers from outside.

"Come on," she said, taking his arm and heading for the French windows, "let's go see what's happening out there!"

If the interior of Mydworth Manor was extravagant, Kat could see from the terrace that the gardens and grounds were going to be even more amazing.

On the small lake behind the house, a pair of gondolas were ferrying couples to and from the little island with its white stone building. It was called a "folly", she knew, though she didn't have a clue why.

A classical string quartet played on the lawn, and an elegant soprano stood with them singing an aria.

"Puccini, if I'm not mistaken," said Harry.

"One of my favourites," said Kat. "First opera ever at The Met… Tosca. Oh – look there. That fire-eater—"

Harry stepped back as a young man, stripped to the waist, twirled into view, shooting flames into the evening sky. A small crowd gathered to watch him.

"Are there clowns and tight-rope walkers due soon? Going to be a long night, I think," said Kat. "Maybe hit the buffet?"

"A very good idea," said Harry.

As they turned to go back indoors, Kat caught a movement in a copse of trees beyond the terrace. A tall, hooded monk, in a long black robe, stood close by another man dressed – she guessed – as Henry VIII, his stomach bulging.

From the finger pointing, and head shakes, the two were clearly arguing, but their voices were low.

Something about the way they stood together made Kat pause for a second. Something… furtive… in their manner. Looking around. Checking.

Almost as if they were hiding.

"You all right?" said Harry.

"Sure," said Kat, turning, and following. "Some of these costumes – crazy, aren't they?"

"YOUR COOK MCLEOD HAS outdone himself tonight, Aunt Lavinia," said Harry, putting down his plate and wiping his hands on a napkin.

Kat looked across, to see Lavinia approaching the corner where she and Harry had perched together to eat.

She thought that amid the sea of cardinals, doges, and even more courtesans and pirates, Lavinia in her gown – a duchess perhaps? – took the cake. Waves of blue material shimmered in the glow of lamps and candles.

"I do *hope* so," Lavinia said. "We've hired God knows how many extra kitchen staff to make sure things roll along. But—"

"Something wrong?" Kat said.

"Well. There are these absolutely darling little lobster things that *should* have arrived by now. I do want to keep my guests well fed."

"Would you like me to go and check the kitchen?" Harry said. "I can be very discreet; they'll never know I'm having a snoop!"

Kat was still getting used to seeing her husband as a pirate, his face hidden by a mask, which she had to admit rendered him even more attractive.

"Would you? I really must circulate among the throng."

Lavinia reached out and touched Kat's forearm. "Some of the people here? I don't even know their names! But invite one from a certain set and you have to invite them all!"

Harry – about to make a run to the downstairs, where mayhem must be reigning in the kitchen – said, "You okay here, Kat? Just a minute or two. On your own?"

"Sure," Kat said. "I'll be fine. After all, I'm a courtesan."

She saw both Harry and his aunt grin at this before hurrying away. She stood there, champagne flute in hand.

All alone.

MURDER WORE A MASK

Though here at Mydworth Manor she felt – in a way – that she was at home too.

She put down her plate and headed in the direction of the ballroom where the band was belting out one of her favourite Cole Porter numbers, *What Is This Thing Called Love.*

HARRY THREADED HIS WAY through the guests who filled the main corridor leading to the hallway, nearly bumping into a hooded monk who scurried past and headed up the stairs to the bedrooms.

Must be one of the London guests, staying over, thought Harry, as he watched the monk disappear along the landing above.

He turned down the corridor that led behind the staircase, dodging incoming footmen and maids, all madly bustling, and then headed down the stone steps to the kitchens.

Years ago, growing up here at Mydworth Manor, these subterranean corridors were his special haunts. The old cook (now long passed) had always been happy to find him a treat, or a mug of cocoa, or a warm corner by the stoves on a freezing winter's day.

All that… helped him get through things.

He tipped his mask up – at least the regular staff would recognise him now and not be upset at the unannounced arrival of someone from "above stairs".

Everywhere he looked there was furious activity: trays of food heading one way, great crates of dirty plates going the other for the kitchen porters to wash.

He sidestepped a pair of footmen carrying an impressive cold salmon on a silver salver, and peered through into the busy kitchen – just as a young man in an ill-fitting footman's uniform bearing a massive bowl of oysters slipped on the wet floor… and fell badly, the bowl flying from his hands and smashing on the hard stone kitchen floor.

For a second there was utter silence. *It was that loud!* Then from every side, Harry saw kitchen staff race to the disaster – some to clear, some to clean.

One figure – the fearsome cook McLeod – picked up the young lad by the shoulder and dragged him to one side, an unintelligible stream of curses echoing around the kitchen.

"What's the bloody point of you, laddie! I'll kick your arse back to that boat you came off—"

Harry stepped forward and McLeod spun round, surprised to see Lady Lavinia's nephew here in the kitchens.

"Sir Harry—"

"Sorry to interrupt, McLeod. But Lady Lavinia was wondering how the lobster hors-d'oeuvres were coming along."

With a reluctant shake, McLeod let go of the footman and he sank back to the floor like an unwanted item of clothing.

"Aye, Sir Harry, should be ready. I'll just away and see," he said, leaving Harry and the young man together.

Harry lifted him up.

"You surviving?" said Harry, noting how nervous the lad seemed. Harry's words brought a smile.

"Just about, sir."

"Bark's worse than his bite. You new?"

"Temporary, sir. Just for tonight. For the party."

"Well, not to worry about that little accident. Happens all the time, night like this. Be forgotten before you know it. Probably already is. Though – I'd not recommend a repeat."

"Thank you, sir."

"McLeod will probably want to dock your pay – best give me your name, I'll see you right tomorrow if he does."

The young man frowned, seeming reluctant to answer.

Strange, thought Harry. *Maybe moonlighting, nervous of getting caught?*

"Come on now, lad. Won't go any further," he said.

"Um… Todd, sir. Charlie Todd."

Harry saw Todd glance anxiously down at the floor – where a clasp knife poked out from beneath a cupboard.

"That yours?" said Harry.

Todd nodded, then reached down, picked it up and pocketed it quickly.

"Must have slipped out. When I fell."

"All right, Todd," said Harry, wondering why a kitchen porter found it necessary to carry a pocket knife.

Maybe for his work on a boat? That might fit. Still…

"Well, as you were."

Harry nodded, and watched Todd return to the kitchen, a nervous glance back in Harry's direction before he disappeared.

Strange, thought Harry. *But then, everything's a little strange tonight.*

He turned and headed back to the party.

3.

DANCE THE NIGHT AWAY

KAT STOOD IN THE corner of the ballroom watching the jazz band – and the amazing singer.

The woman was dressed in a sleek red, low-cut evening gown, white silk gloves above her elbows, her whole performance sultry and slick.

Whoever she was, she was clearly a star, and as she sang she moved sinuously in front of the band. Kat could sense not only every man's eye in the room upon her, but every woman's as well.

Totally compelling.

As Kat watched, a tall man in the menacing black costume of – what? An undertaker? Executioner? – came up with the direct stride of someone who had been maybe waiting for *just* the right opportunity.

His mask was a hard white shell, formed into long cheeks and a grotesque hooked nose.

"Ah," the man said beneath the mask, "you must be… *the American girl*, hmm?"

Kat saw the man's dark eyes, but the rubbery protrusion completely covered the rest of his face. He could be anybody, but some instinct told her, he was not anyone she had met before.

She started to answer, finding the term he used repellent on a number of fronts.

"Oh, excuse my manners," he said, leaning closer. "I meant... the new Lady Mortimer."

He then gave a short bow that – in his sombre outfit – looked like it could have been sarcastic.

"And I have the pleasure of talking to... not a clown, I guess?" she said.

The man produced a small laugh.

"No. Not this evening. In fact, *The Plague Doctor*, at your service."

"Remind me never to catch the plague," said Kat.

The man laughed again, and raised his mask slightly: "Touché. Cyril Palmer, MP." Then as if the "American girl" had just arrived on these shores, "Member of Parliament. In the cabinet actually. All such very dreary stuff to talk about, especially at a lively affair like this one."

She wanted to inform the man that she wasn't the one that brought up the subject of the cabinet and his role therein.

"Enjoying the band?" he said, looking across the ballroom at them.

"Extraordinary singer."

"Isn't she? Celine Dubois. Taking London's theatres by storm this summer. Such a charming young thing. And that voice? Remarkable."

"You know her?"

"As an MP," he said with a shrug, "one tends to know *anyone* who's anyone."

"I'm sure," said Kat, thinking about making her escape from this self-important boor.

"And your husband? Sir Harry? Old boy gone missing, has he? How very careless of him."

Kat managed a polite smile.

"Just checking on the waves of seafood set to arrive."

"Ah. Bit understaffed tonight, hmm? I always say, that if you deign to throw a 'do' such as this, you'd better—"

Then like a rescue boat arriving in the nick of time, shark circling, Harry – her pirate – reappeared.

"Sir Harry?" said Palmer.

Kat waited to see if Harry knew this man.

"Why, yes. And you? With the mask and all—"

And at that, Kat saw Cyril Palmer, MP, tilt up his bizarre mask with its lengthy curved nose.

"Ah. Palmer." Harry stuck out a hand to shake.

"Been a while, eh, Sir Harry? Heard you were doing quite a bit of travelling. Acquiring the odd treasure, here and there, I imagine."

And without Harry saying a word, she could tell, yes, Harry knew the man.

And didn't particularly like him.

He managed a grin.

"Doing my best to keep the empire intact. So far-flung, you know? Perhaps you people in the government should look into consolidating the damn thing."

Kat didn't see a matching smile on Palmer's face. She guessed: jokes about the "empire" were not everyone's cup of tea.

"I was just telling your lovely um… Lady Mortimer here, about my work in parliament. Busy, busy, as they say."

Harry fired a look at Kat.

"I heard your star is in ascent. Rumblings of a run for prime minister?"

"Oh, don't believe everything you hear. Though with the way things are being messed up these days, no doubt a hand like mine at the tiller could—"

"Oh, *so* sorry—" Harry said, cutting him off. "I see some old friends. Been a lifetime. Must catch up, introduce them to Lady Mortimer."

"Why, yes, of course."

And without allowing the now stumbling Cyril Palmer to continue, Harry guided her away.

"SORRY, ABOUT THAT, KAT. Parties like this, you can never tell what piece of flotsam or jetsam you might bump into."

"Got the feeling he waited until I was alone."

"Really? Now why ever would a man like *that* wait till the most beautiful woman in the room was alone to make his move?"

Kat laughed and affected the accent of a southern belle. "Why I do declare, Sir Harry."

"Now whatever is *that* supposed to mean!" he said, laughing as – with a tray soaring by – he scooped up two more glasses of champagne.

"Chin-chin," he said as they toasted. "I'm not sure what that means either."

Kat's eye had been drifting to the fireplace.

It was the Henry VIII that she'd noticed in the garden, and next to him – Kat guessed from her days attending mass at St Brendan's – was a Venetian altar boy.

The masked monarch was gesturing, pointing at the people standing by him, who all listened intently as if his words were important.

"Harry. Don't turn and look right now. But you see Henry VIII over there, holding court?"

And she saw Harry slowly turn, a quick look, and then back to Kat.

"Him? Oh yes, *very* important man. Horatio Forsyth. Publishes one of London's biggest papers, *The Record.*"

"And the choirboy?"

"Ha, anything but. Name's Quiller – gossip columnist. Exposés, and all that. Scourge of half the people in this room."

"Nasty," said Kat.

"Very, so I hear."

"Quite a crowd around them though?"

"Well, with a newspaper empire behind you, people tend to listen even if what you say is complete nonsense!"

Kat took another sip of champagne, enjoying this game of observations.

As she again scanned the room, she saw Celine Dubois at the centre of another group, smoking a cigarette in a holder.

"What do you think of our singer? Striking outfit, and seems to have a real fan following. Least with the men."

"Hmm… let me see," said Harry. "Ah, yes! The beautiful Celine Sawyer."

"Not Dubois?"

"*Think* that's her stage name. Maiden name, probably. She's married to the cinema actor—?"

"Nick Sawyer? Really? I've seen his films. Robin Hood, yes?"

"Yes, that's the one, ever the swashbuckler. In fact, I do believe that's *him,* over there by the drinks."

Kat looked across to the long table of champagne glasses, staffed by busy footmen.

A slender and rather handsome man – dressed as Valentino in a bullfighter's cape – was leaning precariously against the table, knocking back a glass of champagne.

"Said star looks rather wobbly," said Kat. "Hope he doesn't try and swing on the chandeliers."

"Indeed," said Harry. "Word is he's hit a bit of a rough patch. What with the advent of the talkies. I'll take you over, introduce you, if you fancy an autograph."

"Lady Mortimer, Sir Harry—"

Kat turned to see Benton, Lady Fitzhenry's butler, holding a tray, a role she knew he must find beneath him.

"Ah yes. You see, Kat, when I went downstairs old McLeod had things well under control. And these, Benton, are-?"

"Lobster cheese *canapés*, Sir Harry," said Benton, trying and failing to hide his discomfort.

"Really?" Then to Kat. "Shall we?"

And she reached up and with one bite she thought, *Lavinia's cook may be a gruff no-nonsense Scot, but if he can whip up dainties like this, well he is some chef.*

Benton sailed away to other guests.

"Harry, does Benton ever break that façade? I'm getting the feeing it's been quite a while since that man has actually smiled."

"Smile? Well – ha – we tend to frown on people in service doing such things. Do wish he'd return with some more of those lobster things though. Quite tasty, and I'm sure my eating's not keeping up with my drinking."

Just then the band struck up again.

"Oh, Harry! Let's dance, shall we? It's been *ages*."

"Love to," said Harry, putting down his glass.

And Kat took Harry's arm and led him to the ballroom.

4.

DEATH IN VENICE

TWO HOURS LATER, Harry and Kat spilled out of the ballroom into one of the lounges, laughing and exhausted.

"Say – let's find somewhere quiet for a minute," said Harry, and they wandered down the corridor. "You've worn me out."

As they passed the billiard room, Kat glanced in. A group of men were playing billiards. Others stood and smoked cigars, watching.

She recognised Palmer, mask now off, standing, chalking a cue. He nodded recognition to her, then crouched to play a shot.

Harry carried on, and she caught up, past other drifting guests, and entered one of the big lounges.

Kat saw the room was nearly empty – most of the guests still dancing to the amazing band. Outside was now dark, apart from the tall flickering flares that lined the edge of the terrace.

"The look on those generals' faces on the dance floor," said Harry, picking up a bottle of champagne and a couple of glasses and steering Kat towards an empty sofa. "That was something close to real fear."

"The Black Bottom," said Kat, leaning on him while she slipped her shoes back on. "My speciality."

"Don't know how I kept up with you – but always great fun trying. You must—"

But then the French windows flew open, banging against the wall like a gunshot. And though in the ballroom the band played on, the whole crowd singing "Tiptoe Through the Tulips", here in this room, the bubbly air of the party quickly changed.

As two people, one wearing a cavalier hat and a black cape, holding the hand of a lithe woman in an orange gown, appeared in the doorway. They took a breathless moment, before yelling, as loud as they could, for all to hear:

"Someone's down at the lake! Not moving!"

For a moment, the other guests in the lounge just gazed at the couple as if they didn't quite understand the words. Kat understood the implication straight away.

Harry turned to her.

"We'd better go look," he said, his voice suddenly coloured by alarm.

To which Kat answered faster than he could dash away, "Come on."

TOGETHER, THEY RAN DOWN the sloping lawn towards the ornamental lake.

Harry saw the gondolas were all now moored by the flare-lit jetty, those flares the only light down here, away from the house, apart from a half-moon above.

Even in the light from that moon, he could see the shape of a man lying face down on the grass by the grotto, itself on the very edge of the water.

He and Kat reached the man together, Kat as ever taking over, crouching down, checking for pulse, breathing – any signs of life.

A year on the Western Front as a nursing assistant, the making of her, he knew.

He helped her to flip the man over.

"Anything?" he said.

He saw her shake her head and sit back on her haunches.

"Who is it?" she said.

Harry gently lifted the man's head so he could see.

Clearly a guest – in monk's dark robes and sandals. But no mask.

A tall man, in his late sixties perhaps.

"I don't know," said Harry. "Though I think I spotted him at the party."

"Me too," said Kat. "He was having an argument with Henry VIII."

"Whoever he is – he's dead."

HARRY HAD – at Sergeant Timms's request – asked all the guests who had filtered down to the lakeside, right near the stone grotto that Harry loved as a child, to return to Mydworth Manor.

Until the only people near the body were his Aunt Lavinia, Kat, Timms and Constable Thomas.

And Cyril Palmer.

Because the man on the ground, mask nowhere to be seen, and monk's cowl removed, was – as Palmer muttered, his voice shaken – one Wilfred Carmody.

Palmer's long-time assistant and secretary, having loyally worked for him for decades.

Dr Creighton Bedell, the town's lone doctor for as long as Harry could remember, had crouched down close, stethoscope out.

The venerable doctor leaving no stone unturned.

MURDER WORE A MASK

Then that fateful shake of his head confirming what Harry thought was clearly obvious.

"The man is, I am afraid, *dead*."

Kat gave Harry's hand a squeeze. With her shoulders exposed, and the night air turning chilly, Harry took off his pirate's cape and wrapped it around her.

"Thanks," Kat said quietly.

"The poor chap," Palmer said, stepping away, as if now thinking it best to keep his distance from his loyal aide.

"I told Carmody… you don't *have* to come to the party. With his condition and all."

Timms walked over, tilted his head back as if the angle would give a better look. Constable Thomas's torch was still aimed at the body and the doctor, who looked like he might have a struggle standing up.

"'Condition' you say, Mr Palmer?"

"His *heart*, sergeant. Been worse lately. Those funny old rumblings."

From near the corpse, Dr Bedell added, "Palpitations?"

"Yes. But dear Carmody, wanted to be at my side. So *bloody* loyal."

Bedell strained to get to a standing position, placing one hand on a knee for leverage.

The mud here was a good half-inch deep – shoes ruined.

"Officer," Bedell said, "please, if you would be so kind as to aim your torch at Mr Carmody's face."

Constable Thomas did so, and Harry saw something that he had seen before.

"Note that bit of colour… at the cheeks… around the mouth?" said Bedell. "Purplish blue. All the signs of drastic heart failure.

The man probably came out here, seeking some air. Then, well, it was his time."

At this, Lavinia took some muddy steps closer.

"Harry. Do you think I should send everyone away?"

Harry looked at Kat, a certain absurd quality to all of them standing out here, by the lake, gathered around an old man felled by his heart.

But before he could answer: "Lady Lavinia, Constable Thomas and I will see to Mr Carmody here," said Timms. If that suits you, Mr Palmer."

"Of course, sergeant," said Palmer. "You'll need to let me check Mr Carmody's pockets too, lest there might be any papers on him. Government business, you know."

"Yes sir," said Timms. Then, turning to Lavinia, "I think m'lady, there's no reason at all to discomfort your guests."

Lavinia still looked at Harry. Waiting on his response.

"Makes sense, Aunt Lavinia. Things like this happen. Party still going strong. So yes, we can soldier on." He looked down to the body in the mud. "Raise a glass to the fallen."

Lavinia nodded, perhaps – Harry thought – relieved. Would be more of a mess to abruptly end things than let the party run on, albeit it at a lower boil.

And then, as they were about to walk back to the manor house, he turned.

To see Kat. Standing quietly, close to the body, looking down. Then around – at the house, the lake, the grotto.

What's my Kat thinking? he wondered.

5.

A MORNING VISIT FROM AUNT LAVINIA

HARRY WAS STILL TRYING to figure out how the various bits and pieces of the percolator came together, when he heard a knock on the front door.

The coffee was much needed on a morning like this, but the knocking was much more demanding than the recalcitrant coffee maker.

He hurried to the door, his dark blue robe open over pyjamas; the belt somehow gone astray, surely to be located later.

"Yes, yes," he said, opening the door a little and peering round – annoyed that the challenge of the coffee pot had to be deferred – to see his Aunt Lavinia, dressed in slacks, a crisp cream-coloured blouse, her hair pinned up, no hat.

Somewhat different from whatever Venetian she was supposed to be the night before.

"Aunt Lavinia. I thought, after last night, and all the aftermath, we wouldn't be seeing you stir till noon."

She made a small smile at that.

And as if to prod – Harry perhaps seeming sluggish though it was hardly the crack of dawn – she said, "Mind if I come in, my dear?"

"Oh, of *course*. I mean, absolutely."

He pulled the door open, adding: "Would you like some tea? Think we have some biscuits from yesterday, and—"

At that, he saw Kat emerge from their bedroom, drawn by the sound. Her silky gown and robe, pulled tight. *Altogether fetching*, he thought, *even the morning after.*

"Aunt Lavinia. Good morning."

"Yes, yes. Harry, now, do see to that tea. And Kat, I'm *so* glad you are up. *Both* of you need to hear what I have to say."

Harry still hadn't moved towards any tea preparations. This visit did not bode well.

"Something else happen last night, Aunt Lavinia? I mean after we left? Seemed that post-Carmody's collapse the party was still going full steam?"

"Yes. Well, bring me that tea and I shall tell you."

KAT WAS PLEASED LAVINIA wanted to share her story with her. Harry's aunt seemed to be – albeit slowly – warming to Kat.

From the look on Lavinia's face, it must be serious.

She sat down in a kitchen chair while Harry wrestled with the electric kettle, a device he was still getting used to. She also noted the dismembered parts of the percolator that, with coffee not being such a priority in this country, he had not yet learned to master.

"Aunt Lavinia, did everyone stay up terribly late?"

"Oh yes, Kat. I mean, not unexpected. Benton and the staff were good enough to stay at their posts until the last house guest retired. The locals stumbled back into town I imagine, while those heading back to London of course left much earlier. I intend to reconsider the whole 'house guest' thing. Such an effort! Must always sort them a bedroom, and one for their staff if they bring any! Feed them on and on, like noisy chicks in a nest."

At that, Lavinia made a small smile. "So much work for such a little party."

Kat smiled back. She had learned that Lavinia – who had raised Harry since he was a small boy – was not unlike her. Strong opinions, but backed with a steely resolve to *get things done*, and more importantly, have a good time doing it, no matter what people might say.

She guessed that attitude was becoming more common in this country, just as back in the States, independent women were popping up all over the place.

Good thing too.

The steady whistle from the nearby kitchen signalled that Harry had the tea well in hand.

He soon appeared with a steaming tea pot, three cups and saucers, and a plate of cookies, biscuits, that Kat hoped hadn't turned too crumbly since yesterday.

"There!" Harry said. "Got the milk and sugar too. Aren't I the domesticated one? Now, Lavinia, while it is always a pleasure to have you visit us, perhaps… to the reason?"

Kat saw Harry's aunt take a deep breath.

"Yes, well – this is what happened…"

"RATHER LATER THAN PLANNED, well after midnight, I had the maids arrange things for that card-hunting game."

"Oh, *that* one. Good fun. Usually."

Kat's confused look to him prompted, "Oh, you see, tradition has it, always a game or two at the end of a party. This one involves a deck of cards, the individual cards secreted around the house."

"Some outside too," Lavinia added.

"And people search high and low, avoiding private areas, of course. Then they can get into teams, and match cards to see—"

"Yes, yes, Harry we don't need *all* the rules for it. And the game is not the important thing."

"Something happened during the game?"

Lavinia fixed her nephew with a stare. "Did you perhaps overdo it a bit last night, Harry?"

"Never a morning person, dear Aunt. So—?"

"Right." And again, she looked straight at Kat. "I wasn't playing the game, just overseeing, when that newspaper publisher—"

"Horatio Forsyth," Harry added. "Henry the Eighth, if I remember correctly."

"Yes. Came up to me. Pulled me aside. I mean, *literally*. His eyes wide. Well, I have seen fear before. And in those eyes… definitely a healthy dose of fear."

Kat noted that Lavinia's words had produced a sudden change in her husband. Lips set, eyes locked on her.

"He walked me – almost dragged me – to the alcove that leads down to the servants' staircase. And then—"

"Go on," said Harry.

"He said he had something important to tell me about Mr Carmody's death."

Kat caught Harry's quick glance across at her.

Serious. Concerned.

"Well, you can imagine how that made me feel," said Lavinia.

And Kat could. One night in Istanbul, she had barely fallen asleep when there was a noise. Someone in her apartment, perhaps having gained entry from the wide-open window, the night hot.

Kat had got up then, heart pounding. Aware that there was *someone there*. That there was now something to fear.

But with the flick of a light, the intruder, knowing that he had been discovered, stumbled out again.

And for the next night, Kat made sure her Colt revolver was just tucked under her bed, a quick and easy grab should she need it.

"Aunt Lavinia, what exactly did Mr Forsyth say? What was he afraid of?" Kat asked.

"He said that — and these are his *precise* words – whoever did that to Carmody knew that he and Carmody were up to something *together*."

"I see," Harry said.

"He also said that whoever did it will be coming for him next!"

"And what was the connection?" said Kat

Lavinia nodded. Took a sip of tea. Then…

"OF COURSE, I STOPPED the man right there. Told him, with all these people staying in my house, best I *didn't* know whatever it was he was referring to. Then I mentioned, well *you two*. Your… special talents in this area."

"And the old newspaper man was fine with that? You telling us?"

"Yes. He definitely did not want the police involved, that's for sure."

"People rarely do, I'm beginning to find."

"Lavinia," Kat said, "you'd like us to look into this?"

At that Lavinia stood up.

"Please. I mean Forsyth may have some dreadful secret. Of course, to any sane person, it would seem that Carmody, with his heart history, simply keeled over. *Quod erat demonstrandum*."

"Still got your Latin, I see," Harry said, now standing as well. Then: "I think – once we've had a bite to eat – we'll be glad to start poking around in things."

"I knew I could rely on you two. Now, I imagine people up at the house will soon start stirring for breakfast. One or two are already out riding. Then I gather there's something of a tennis tournament scheduled."

She took Kat's hand.

"You play, yes, Kat? Perhaps you will join us? Might prove useful."

Kat smiled. "Certainly."

"Let's not forget that I, too, know how to wield a racquet," Harry said.

And at that finally Lavinia managed a relieved smile.

"Of *course* you do, dear Harry. I must tell you both," she said, as she turned headed for the front door, "you agreeing to do this, why already it's a tremendous load off my shoulders."

"Glad to help," Harry said, hurrying to open the door for his aunt.

"Now back to my house full of people. Still so many people."

And Kat watched as Lavinia made her way round the side of the Dower House to the winding country path that connected the two homes.

Could have taken the car, Kat thought.

But then… people noticing, asking questions.

This way, nice and tidy and secret.

One savvy woman.

Then as Harry shut the door.

"What do you think, Sir Harry?"

"I think – Lady Mortimer – we may just have another case to solve."

"A case of… murder?"

"*That* remains to be seen. Now please, can your more experienced hands wrestle the percolator into submission? And then we'll get cracking."

6.

FOOTSTEPS ON THE GRASS

KAT REACHED OUT AND stopped Harry just as he was about to open the grand front door to Mydworth Manor.

"Harry, how about – before we talk to Forsyth – we go take a look, down where the grotto is? I mean, last night no one was thinking anything. Now—"

"In the light of day, a hint of suspicion in the air?"

"*Exactly!*"

"Lead on."

They walked around the house and took the gravel path down to where a lush green carpet of grass hugged close to the small lake, just north of the main grounds, leading to the grotto.

HARRY KNELT DOWN, looking at the churned-up mud at the water's edge made by all the people who had stomped about here last night.

He looked up at Kat. "Going to take Grayer quite a bit of work to get this patch looking like it hasn't been turned into cow pasture."

He saw Kat looking around, to the east where the lake ended and the grass trailed off into the rising hills where Harry had loved to play when he was young.

He and his pals would run around, playing at being soldiers as they hid behind giant rocks and climbed trees – not knowing that, for nearly all of them, the real thing was not too far away.

And that only a few would return.

Kat turned and looked back to where they had come from.

"You, m'lady, are having some thoughts, yes?"

She nodded. "That I am. I mean, this grotto, it's a long way from the house."

"Yes, I suppose it is. Bit of a refuge. Sit there, book of poetry in your lap. Rather peaceful, don't you think?"

"Yes, but that's just it."

Kat, seemingly unconcerned that her leather laced-up boots were turning a darker brown as they sank into the mud, took a step towards him.

"Go on," said Harry.

Another step. And now with the late morning sun hitting his wife squarely in her face, making each angle stand out, her blue eyes glistening, she faced him directly and said, "That's just it. Carmody, maybe not feeling all that well, wants some air. But why on earth…?"

"Walk this far?"

"*Precisely*. It's a long walk from the party in the dark. Especially when you're not feeling well."

"Doesn't add up."

"No, it doesn't."

"Suspicious?"

At that Kat shrugged. "Curious. Odd. No easy explanation."

"Well, we are a little early in this investigation."

"Is that what it is?"

"Time will tell, my dear, but… hang on…"

"What?"

Harry had noticed something, the sun at a high enough angle that he could make out the ripples and lines in the churned-up mud.

"Do step carefully for a minute. But follow me."

He stepped over the mess of jumbled footprints to where he saw just *one* set of footprints. He stopped and Kat followed suit.

"Harry, what is it?"

He pointed where the footprints led away from the muddy jumble.

"Notice anything?"

Kat paused, right at his shoulder. "These prints here. One set. Heading off in *that* direction, away from us. Not directly back to the house."

"Unlike the other ones," he said.

"Yes. So who would do that, with the body on the ground, and the police on the scene? No one could just walk away, unnoticed. Someone would have seen them. Don't you think?"

Harry stood up.

"That I do. Which means—"

"The footsteps were made *before* anyone discovered the body of Wilfred Carmody."

"Makes sense," he said. "But I'd wager if we follow the prints, they'll disappear as soon as we get away from the mud, and onto the grass. Then… who knows where they went?"

He watched Kat scan the lake, the grass, then back to the grotto.

"It might also mean," she said, "that when Carmody came down here, he was *not* alone."

"He came down here to meet somebody."

"Exactly," Kat said. "You know, for a warm morning, that thought just gave me quite a chill."

"Me too, I must admit. Though quite how you give someone a heart attack on cue…"

"Can be done," said Kat, her face now serious. "So I've heard."

Harry nodded, knowing that Kat, in her years working for the American government, had experience of the darker side of the diplomatic arts.

As indeed had he, in service with His Majesty's Diplomatic Corps.

"In which case, perhaps I should phone Dr Bedell, ask him to take a discreet look at the body."

"And order an autopsy."

"That too," said Harry, "but in the meantime, worth a careful inspection here for signs of anything untoward."

"I agree," said Kat. "You know, I just remembered something from last night. Not sure it's important."

"I'm sure it is," said Harry.

He looked at Kat, the morning sun catching her hair.

This conversation so incongruous.

"Just after we arrived, I saw Forsyth arguing with someone out on the lawn. Someone in a monk's robe, like Carmody's."

"Funny you say that," said Harry. "*I* saw a monk in a hurry on the staircase last night. Course, always hard to tell one monk from another. And in a mask, well…"

"Perfect set-up to kill somebody, wouldn't you say? Masks, disguises…"

"Indeed," he said, wiping his muddy shoes against the grass. "Well this idea of yours – coming down here – jolly productive. Shall we see the state of play up at the house?"

"By all means."

And Harry walked beside Kat.

For now they were silent, though he guessed she had to be thinking the same as him.

What on earth actually happened last night?

Had Carmody been murdered?

If so, why?

And how?

KAT FOLLOWED HARRY UP the steps onto the rear terrace of Mydworth Manor, and through the French windows into the house.

She could see that the staff had already been busy cleaning and tidying. Last night's Venetian decorations were all gone, and the floors looked freshly swept and polished.

Maids and footmen – *they had to be weary!* – still scurried back and forth, carrying trays – presumably for those guests still in their bedrooms.

She and Harry walked down the corridor into the big living room. A handful of overnight guests sat on sofas and armchairs – some stood in the open French windows.

Everyone was now in their normal weekend clothes – Venetian costumes gone.

She saw Benton delivering drinks on a tray to one couple she did recognise, standing just outside on the terrace: Celine Dubois and her husband Douglas Sawyer.

As Benton came back through the living room, Harry nodded to him.

"Benton."

"Sir Harry?"

"People still having breakfast?"

"Yes, sir, though many of her ladyship's guests have preferred breakfast in their rooms."

"I can imagine why, eh? Mr Palmer down yet?"

"Indeed yes, sir, he was one of the first to arise. I gather he is out riding sir."

"Nothing gets in the way of an Englishman and his morning ride," said Harry.

"What about Mr Forsyth?" said Kat.

"Still in his room, I believe, Lady Mortimer. He was one of the last to take to his bed last night, what with the… er… unfortunate incident by the lake."

"Of course," said Kat. "Seems he was pretty upset." Then a thought: "I wonder – don't suppose you know if anyone in particular left very muddy shoes out last night to be cleaned?"

"Muddy shoes, m'lady? It is more a question of who *didn't* do so. The lakeside entertainments, while being of course a marvellous diversion, have taken their toll on the carpets and footwear *throughout* the house."

So much for identifying the mystery footprints this morning, thought Kat.

"Well, we won't delay you much more, Benton," said Harry. "Just one last question…" Kat saw him nod to the Sawyers through the French windows. "That a brandy you were just pouring for Mr Sawyer?"

"It was indeed, sir," said Benton, heading back towards the kitchens.

"The old eye-opener," said Harry. "Thought Sawyer looked two sheets to the wind last night."

"Me too," said Kat. "Know what? Might be a long wait for Forsyth to emerge, why don't we start talking to people, see if anyone knows anything?"

"Good idea. Fancy the singer and the silent movie star?"

"You know me too well. How about you?"

"Think I'll take a quiet peek at Carmody's room."

"Really?" said Kat.

"I was thinking – remember last night Palmer mentioned important papers? Carmody's been Palmer's private secretary for years. Could be that Palmer trusted him with information that might have put him in harm's way."

"Government secrets, you mean? Always possible. Though perhaps political secrets are more likely," she said.

"Good point – Palmer running for Number Ten this autumn. Even people on his own side of the House might be interested in what he's up to."

"Journalists too," said Kat.

"Newspaper barons, even…" said Harry, smiling.

"Maybe a good idea then to search Carmody's room before Palmer's back from his ride," said Kat. "Meanwhile, I'm going to grab a coffee and get the latest gossip from Hollywood."

"Think I got the raw deal there," said Harry, giving her a kiss on the cheek. "Love you."

Kat watched him head off to look for Benton, and then went looking for a coffee.

Maybe there was more to Mr Carmody than we thought.

7.

THE SINGER AND THE STAR

HARRY WALKED QUIETLY ALONG the second-floor corridor until he reached Carmody's room – one of the small singles up here not allocated to servants.

He tapped quietly on the door – though he knew it was unoccupied. Then he took from his pocket the spare key he'd got from Mrs Woodfine, the housekeeper, slipped it in the lock – and entered.

Mrs Woodfine had assured him that absolutely no one had been in here since Carmody himself.

"That Mr Palmer, sir, he asked me last night if I could open the room up for him, but I said only you or Lady Fitzhenry or the police could do that. I hope that was right, sir?"

Harry had assured her she'd done the correct thing – spot on – and also that he'd do his best to retrieve the proper key from Mr Carmody, *"otherwise we'll be a key short, sir, and that's not right".*

Inside, the heavy, dark curtains were drawn. He shut the door behind him, went to open them, then turned to survey the room.

First look: Carmody was clearly tidy – no surprise there, for a man who had devoted his life to being a secretary.

A single bed, pyjamas folded atop the pillow.

Though, sadly, never to be worn by their owner again.

A wardrobe. Wash-stand. A small desk, a leather briefcase upon it. A copy of Dickens' David Copperfield on the bedside table. A luggage rack, with a weekend bag buckled tight.

Harry went to the wardrobe, opened it. Evening dress, shoes, coat. Harry checked the pockets, finding nothing.

Carefully, he went through the rest of the room, opening the drawers, searching pockets.

The briefcase did indeed contain papers. Harry reached across, clicked on the small electric desk lamp, then took out the papers, piled them on the desk and set about looking them over.

All clearly government papers, and probably private. But Harry – in his discreet "back-office" role at the Foreign Office – knew that he was cleared to read just about anything here that might catch his interest…

… if he considered that the security of the country might be at risk.

One never knows such things, Harry thought as he began scanning the stack of papers.

"CHAPLIN?" SAID DOUGLAS SAWYER, pouring the dregs of his brandy into his coffee and swigging the lot down. "Overblown. Opinionated. And not nearly as funny in real life as one might imagine. Tedious fellow, if you ask me."

"Really?" said Kat, watching as Sawyer flapped his hand to attract the attention of a passing footman and order another drink.

Although from a distance he looked every bit the romantic lead – tall, dark eyes, loose-limbed – now close, this morning Kat could see his skin had a sweaty pallor, and those eyes were horribly bloodshot.

And his voice – too high, almost squeaky – incongruous for a screen idol famous for action roles and heroic yarns.

"Douglas doesn't have much time for slapstick – do you, darling?" said Celine, drawing elegantly on her cigarette holder then tapping the ash onto the terrace next to her steamer chair.

"Too right! Pratfalls are hardly our greatest contribution to the dramatic arts," said Sawyer, one eye on the French windows for any sign of his approaching refill.

Although it was already warm out here on the terrace, Kat felt that maybe Harry got the better deal out of the two detective tasks this morning.

All the Sawyers had done since she'd joined them for coffee was snipe at each other – or about other entertainers.

Talk about tedious.

She looked across the terrace to the lawns and the distant woods. Someone she recognised was walking across the grass towards the house: the journalist who'd been at Forsyth's side the night before, while the publisher was holding forth.

Quiller – was that his name?

She felt that maybe she would learn more talking to him – not this tetchy pair.

She turned back to the couple and smiled.

Sawyer seemed more than bitter, almost angry. Celine also was touchy – hard to remember the beauty of her voice from the night before – as she did nothing to hide her irritation with her husband.

Perhaps news of the death of Carmody had affected them, Kat thought. But something was certainly rattling both of them.

If so, what?

Time to move the conversation on.

"Do you mind if I ask you about Wilfred Carmody?" said Kat. "The man who died last night."

"Didn't put a damper on the old party, now did it?" said Sawyer. Then Kat saw his eyes narrow. "What's your question?"

"Terrible thing to happen, out there all alone," said Kat, thinking fast. "We, all of us, wonder if perhaps we should have seen the signs, got the poor man to take it easy, call a doctor, you know?"

"Heart attack, wasn't it?" said Sawyer. "They can come out of the blue, you know. And bang! You're a goner, right? Seems pretty cut and dried to me."

Kat nodded, then waited as a footman appeared and replaced the actor's brandy.

"Not much you can do if your number's up," said Sawyer, taking a gulp.

"Did you know him?"

"Carmody? Me? Why should I? Never clapped eyes on him in my life."

"Hmm, not *strictly* true, Douglas darling," said Celine, with a condescending smile.

Kat could see little affection in those eyes.

"What do you mean?" said Sawyer, face flushing. "I can assure you, I never met the chap!"

"You forget. Must be the brandies, hmm?" said Celine. Then she turned to Kat. "Douglas and I took the White Star to New York last year."

"Film offer, don't you know," said Sawyer.

Celine carried on, not glancing at him. "We had the pleasure of dining with Cyril Palmer at the Captain's table."

Kat heard Sawyer give a dismissive grunt at her side.

"Palmer, right. Yes, I do remember that. God, what a bore he was."

"In fact," said Celine, ignoring her husband. "I do believe we played bridge with him and Mr Carmody, who was travelling with him as a kind of aide-de-camp."

"Really?" said Sawyer. "Seems it wasn't *all* that memorable, darling." The actor swirled his glass, now holding only melted ice cubes. "Least for me."

So that's how they met, thought Kat. Maybe easily forgotten.

But maybe not.

"And did Mr Carmody appear fit and well?" said Kat.

"Bloody hell. What? Can't even picture the old sod. But you know, he's got a few years on Palmer. Old is old, Lady Mortimer. Sad truth," said Sawyer, beneath his breath.

Kat saw Celine take a deep breath as if not pleased with her husband, then turn back to her.

"As *I* recall, it was not a wonderful crossing for Douglas, Lady Mortimer. My husband, you see, had a bad back the whole voyage," she said. "All those stunts over the years for the cinema. Always proving things! And then when we got to New York, we heard the picture was canned."

Kat heard Sawyer grunt at the memory.

"And what about Mr Carmody?" she said. "You haven't seen him since then?"

"I don't believe so," said Celine. "Apart from last night of course."

Kat caught a look from Sawyer to his wife.

He doesn't trust her one bit, she thought. *So, what's been going on here? Maybe there was something useful to mine from this conversation.*

"This Carmody chap – he got family?" said Sawyer, his voice now slightly slurred.

"Not that anyone's aware of," said Kat, not sure what Sawyer's sudden interest might mean. "Mr Palmer plans on handling all the arrangements."

She waited for another question, but he just nodded and took another sip of his brandy.

Behind them, Kat saw Quiller go through the French windows and disappear into the breakfast room.

"Any particular reason you're interested in Mr Carmody, Lady Mortimer?" said Celine. A small smile. "Just curious."

"Oh, nothing really. I just feel, you know, responsible in some way," said Kat. "That we all let him down."

"Oh, I absolutely understand," said Celine. Then, with a sniff, "But really, you shouldn't blame yourself, none of us should. I'm sure there was nothing anyone could have done to prevent his death."

Kat nodded. Celine seeming so sincere.

Almost too sincere.

"I'm sure you're right," said Kat.

Not sure at all.

"Well, then – unless there's anything else we can help you with…?" said Celine, nodding towards the lawn where Kat now saw Grayer the gardener heading past carrying nets. "I do believe they're setting up for tennis. Will you be playing later?"

"Love the game. Try keeping me away," said Kat, smiling.

"*That's* the spirit," said Celine. "I know – let's partner for the doubles! Hands across the Ocean, hmm?"

"Love to," said Kat. "Now, forgive me while I go see if there's any more coffee in the breakfast room."

She got up, thinking – *some tricky web of connections to unpick here. And could the husband and wife be any more prickly with each other?*

But a bigger question: *does it have anything to do with Carmody?*

MURDER WORE A MASK

Perhaps the young journalist might be able to fill in some of the blanks.

8.

THE DANGEROUS SECRET OF WILFRED CARMODY

HARRY TURNED OVER THE last paper in the pile and sat back in the small chair, arms folded, thinking.

Most of what he'd read had been quite dull correspondence back and forth between Palmer and his constituents, business connections, or fellow parliamentarians.

And although there were some confidences, and a handful of references which might perhaps prove a tad embarrassing to the government, there was nothing that he could see to warrant murder.

No smoking gun.

And before he'd left last night, Sergeant Timms had confirmed that Carmody's pockets were empty.

So, *if* Forsyth was right, and the man's death *wasn't* accidental – then either there were no secrets involved in this affair, or the culprit had taken them away.

In which case, they were probably destroyed by now.

Any trail erased.

He started to slide the papers back in the briefcase – when the door suddenly opened.

"What the hell—?"

Harry turned, to see Cyril Palmer standing, hand still on the doorknob, riding crop in the other hand, his face livid.

"Ah," said Harry. "Mr Palmer."

"If you've been reading my private papers, you'd better have a bloody good explanation, Mortimer."

Harry stood up. "As matter of fact, I do have an explanation. Perhaps you could close the door, sir, and hear me out."

He waited while Palmer shut the door behind him and stepped into the room, his riding jacket and boots giving him an almost military air.

"This had better be *damned* good," said the MP. "Those papers – top government security."

Considering the mundane nature of the documents, Harry thought this was a bit of an overreaction.

Harry leaned back against the desk, wondering how much to reveal of Forsyth's claim that the cause of Carmody's death had been no heart attack.

A claim, so far, without any evidence.

"You see, Palmer, it's been suggested – by one of my aunt's guests – that Carmody's death just might not be as accidental as first appeared."

"What?"

"Indeed, there's a suggestion that Carmody may have been involved in something that got him killed."

"Good God, man. Old Carmody? Some kind of... spy? Is that what you mean?"

"'Spy' perhaps not the right word. But passing on information."

"About *me*? Political information?"

Harry shrugged: "That – afraid I don't know. I had hoped I might find a clue here, in his room."

"All sounds terribly dubious. And what qualifies you to be the judge of that?"

"As I believe you know, I have a position at the Foreign Office. My security clearance is all in order."

"Ah yes. You work for Sinclair's nasty little outfit, don't you?" said Palmer, with what Harry guessed was a tone of distaste. "All spies and secrets? Enough said, dear boy."

Harry had long suspected that his boss's remit – and therefore his own – within the diplomatic service, was probably an open secret within government circles.

"I'm not acting now in an official capacity, of course," said Harry. "But still, a disturbing allegation like that? One can't be too careful."

"Of course," said Palmer, softening. "But – you know – Carmody's been my man for *years*. A damned loyal servant, I'd wager my life on that."

"I'm sure you're right. And so – hear me out – perhaps there's no better way to prove that than by helping me now? These papers, for instance – anything missing?"

Harry waited while Palmer picked up the pile of papers and thumbed through them.

Not happy about any of this, Harry noted. *But at least he's doing it.*

KAT WENT INTO THE breakfast room, poured herself another coffee and looked around. There were still some late risers enjoying breakfast, chattering together at the long table. Seated in an armchair in the far corner, away from the other guests sat Quiller, a pile of newspapers in front of him on a low table.

She walked over.

"Mr Quiller?" she said.

She saw Quiller look up, his eyes lizard-like, slow.

But intense. Penetrating.

"Yes?"

Kat gestured to the armchair next to him.

"May I join you?"

She watched as he seemed to consider the merits of this. Then he shrugged.

"Yes," he said. "But not here. Let's go outside."

He got up, tucked the newspapers under his arm, and headed out of the French windows onto the terrace.

Kat followed and watched him select a table at the end, far away from any other guests.

She sat, put down her coffee.

"You want to ask me about Carmody," said the journalist, "right?"

For a second Kat was taken by surprise.

"Well, I'm not sure I—"

"I assume Forsyth has enlisted your services?"

"He had some concerns, about Mr Carmody's death."

"Quite understandable. The circumstances are suspicious."

"You don't buy the doctor's diagnosis?"

"I wasn't there, Lady Mortimer. But I happen to know that Mr Carmody was in a *vulnerable* position."

"Vulnerable? In what way?"

But she saw Quiller wasn't going to answer that straight away. He took out a cigarette case, and she waited while he lit a cigarette and inhaled.

"You and your husband are getting quite a reputation for this amateur 'sleuthing', aren't you?"

"I really couldn't say."

"It's rather a good story, isn't it? Perhaps I should write it."

"I'm sorry?"

"Your story, *Kat Reilly*."

"I don't have a story."

"But you do. Imagine this: daughter of Bronx barman teams up with English aristo to solve crimes. The Bargirl and the Baronet. Oh, I *like* that. I could sell that."

"Mr Quiller, I'm just an average woman—"

"*Do* come on, Lady Mortimer. Hardly average. And now I come to think on it, your father wasn't *just* a barman, was he? Spent time in jail himself, didn't he?"

Kat took a deep breath. This interview was going nowhere she'd expected. Quiller knew far more about her past than she could have imagined.

"He did. And that's no secret. Early days of prohibition. Happened to a lot of hardworking people. Not a crime in my book."

"Oh, very good. 'Not a crime', the Lady says. I must remember that. I'll use it."

"You can have it," she said, smiling, but inside feeling daggers. "For free."

Kat stared at Quiller, telling herself to stay calm and not rise to the bait.

"Can I get you another coffee?" she said, rising from the table.

"Oh – interview not over?"

Apparently Quiller thought he had adequately rattled her.

Guess what? I don't rattle so easily, thought Kat.

"Not quite."

"Gosh, you Americans. So relentless," Quiller said, doing his best to mimic a New York accent.

Does the word "loathe" apply here? Kat wondered.

"Aren't we just," she said.

Kat picked up her cup and headed back to the breakfast room, trying to figure out how to break through this man's defences.

What's his weakness? Maybe... flattery?

Worth trying.

"ALL PRETTY LOW-GRADE stuff to be honest," said Palmer, putting the pile down a couple of minutes later. "What about the rest of the room? Anything?"

"Not so far. But perhaps you can help me?"

Together they checked absolutely everywhere in the room, lifting the pillows, mattress, emptying and re-packing Carmody's weekend bag.

"That's it, I think?" said Palmer.

Harry looked around the room.

"I believe so."

He watched as Palmer picked up the copy of *David Copperfield* and flicked through it.

"This one? Tad 'heart on the sleeve' for me," said Palmer. "Not big on blatant sentimentality. Though credit to old Dickens – he gets parliament right. Wait. Hang on—"

Harry watched as an envelope fluttered to the ground at Palmer's feet. The MP reached down, picked it up and removed a single sheet of paper from the envelope.

"Good *God*," he said. Then he handed it to Harry, who read it out loud.

"Meet me by the grotto at midnight, to learn urgent things that will be to your advantage. A friend."

"What on earth does this mean?" said Palmer.

"It means, I'm afraid, that – quite likely – our suspicions are right. Carmody's death *wasn't* accidental."

"God, you mean the man was murdered?"

Harry nodded. "Could be. But to prove that, I'm afraid we are going to need more than this note."

"You'd best keep it, Sir Harry," Palmer said, suddenly compliant, his edge gone. "I mean, for your investigation. You'll need it."

Harry held his hand out for the envelope, and Palmer, after a pause, handed it over. Then Harry folded the note, put it in the envelope and slipped it in his jacket pocket.

9.

A REASON TO MURDER

KAT RETURNED TO THE table on the terrace, Quiller sitting, legs crossed, chin resting on one hand.

Supercilious, that's the word to describe him, thought Kat. *Louche. But also – perhaps – dangerous.*

She sat, placed her coffee on the table.

"Of course, Mr Quiller, if you wanted to tell my life story, you'd need me as a consultant."

"Unpaid, you mean?" he said, looking surprised.

"*Unpaid*? I don't think so," she said, smiling.

"Oh, you *are* something special, aren't you?" he said, smiling back.

"You scratch my back."

"Even a Lady needs a little pocket money?" he said.

"Always. And of course, if ever Sir Harry and I come across any little society snippets that you might find useful…"

"Well then, I'm sure a fee can be found," said Quiller.

"I prefer 'like for like'," said Kat. "Cash is so vulgar."

"Can be arranged. Knowledge is power, as somebody once said."

"I think you'll find it was Francis Bacon."

"Touché. Imagine that! A Yank teaching me my own history."

Though Kat was spinning him a line, she suddenly thought – a well-placed, unscrupulous newspaper hack might in fact be useful to have in her pocket.

Never know when a journalist might come in handy.

And though she had disliked the man instantly, when did that ever get in the way of a straightforward business arrangement?

"Back to Mr Carmody. You were going to tell me more," said Kat.

"Um, sorry," said Quiller. "No can do."

"But you know something?"

"That I do. But at the moment, you see, I'm running on Mr Forsyth's meter – not yours."

"So, let me guess. You *were* doing something with Carmody?" said Kat. Then she realised. "No, wait, oh I get it! You were on *Palmer's* case. That right?"

"No comment."

Kat laughed.

"Fair enough. Guess we'll just have to talk to your boss the organ-grinder."

"You'll be lucky," said Quiller. "Forsyth's barricaded himself in his room, from what I gather. Terrified the killer's going to strike again."

"But you're not scared too?"

"I'm just the messenger. Contrary to popular belief, in my experience messengers don't often get shot."

Kat took a sip of coffee, then changed tack.

"You write gossip columns, society articles, yes?"

"Please, Lady Mortimer. I'm a respected investigative journalist."

"Oh, my apologies. Of course. You just happen to spend your life at society events among the rich and famous… who often turn out to be scandalous as well."

"It's where the *stories* are."

"And did you find any stories here last night?"

At that, Quiller paused. His guard quickly back up.

"Nothing I didn't know already."

"Such as?"

Quiller smiled.

She watched him scan the other guests sitting further down the terrace, then the ones back in the breakfast room. Then he turned back to her, his eyes gleaming, as if with the pleasure of the secrets he held.

"The Sawyers," he said, nodding discreetly to where the couple sat some twenty yards away.

"Yes?"

"Dear Douglas – once the darling of housewives worldwide – has just been summarily dropped by his studio."

"Really?"

"Celine doesn't know yet. Idiot hasn't told her. Hence the regular glasses of fortifying spirits which – so far – do not seem to be working."

"Why's he been dropped? I thought he was a big star."

"*Was* is the operative word. You heard him speak?"

"Oh, right. A little thin, squeaky…"

"*Exactly*. This is the age of the talkies. Heroes have to sound like heroes."

"I thought they could fix that in the recording."

"Oh, they might," said Quiller. "Fixing the shakes? That's a little harder."

"Likes his drink a bit too much, huh?"

"Not all he likes, if the rumours are right."

"Dope too?" said Kat.

"You didn't hear it from me."

"Serious?"

A nod. "Word is, yes."

"Does Celine know about that?"

"Doubt she could miss it. But also doubt she's bothered, the circles she moves in," said Quiller, taking out a cigarette case and lighting up. "Very tolerant crowd. Debauched, some might call it. Be a different kettle of fish when she hears he's blown the movie career."

"She'll walk out on him?"

"For sure."

"For somebody else?"

"For Palmer of course."

"But she hardly knows him."

"My dear Kat – may I call you that? – half London knows the pair of them have been at it like rabbits all year. It's an open secret."

"Otherwise you wouldn't be telling me?"

"Exactly."

Kat sat back in her chair.

So, the dancing on the ship had led to trysts in London. Celine had lied to her about hardly knowing Palmer.

Not surprising, given that her husband was in the room. But she had told that bare-faced lie with ice-cold skill.

Something to keep in mind.

And on top of everything, Sawyer was a drug addict whose life was about to blow apart.

She looked down the terrace to where the Sawyers still sat.

Celine was looking straight back at her.

Staring.

Kat smiled and nodded to the singer, but Celine's expression didn't alter. If anything, it hardened.

Uh-oh, thought Kat. *Looks like she knows Quiller's dealing me the dirt.*

She turned back to the journalist.

"Did you see Carmody at all last night?" she said. "Dressed as a monk."

"Of course I did," said Quiller, after a pause. "Well... across the room."

"Did you talk to him?"

Again, another pause.

"No."

"You didn't notice him looking unwell?"

"No."

"Or going outside?"

"I saw him heading upstairs, at one point. Think that's the last time."

"Anyone else look suspicious? Out here in the grounds? Later?"

Kat saw Quiller pause again, frown.

"You might be on Forsyth's dollar, Mr Quiller," said Kat, "but if this does turn into an official police investigation you're going to have to reveal what you saw."

Quiller stubbed out his cigarette – then Kat saw him look around, as if to check again that nobody was eavesdropping.

"All right," he said. "But this didn't come from me, you hear?"

"Go on."

"About eleven, party going strong, I came outside, onto the lawns."

"A little snooping, hmm?"

"I prefer to think of it as *taking the temperature of the party.* Anyway. Pretty dark, not much of a moon. Flares all dying down, you know.

And across the terrace – right here where we're sitting – I saw the Plague Doctor – scurry across, head down, walking fast towards the lake."

"The Plague Doctor. You mean Palmer?"

Quiller shrugged: "Far as I know – he was the only Plague Doctor invited."

Kat stared at him.

"You realise what you're suggesting?"

"I'm not 'suggesting' anything. I'm just saying what I saw."

Kat looked away, thinking.

Palmer the MP, Palmer the possible future Prime Minister, had gone down to the lake at just the time when his private secretary had died in mysterious circumstances.

"Did you tell Mr Forsyth what you saw?"

"Sorry. No comment."

No wonder Quiller was being circumspect about what he said.

And no surprise either that Forsyth had locked himself in his room.

Palmer was one of the most powerful people in the country.

Was it possible that he was involved in Carmody's death?

Or worse…

Had Palmer himself actually murdered him?

HARRY CAME DOWN THE small staircase to the first floor, having left Palmer to change out of his riding gear.

He needed to find Kat, tell her about the mysterious assignation.

But first, perhaps Forsyth was finally up and about?

He walked along the landing, past the main guest rooms, then stopped at what he knew from Benton was Forsyth's room.

Tapped on the door. No answer.

"Mr Forsyth? Mr Forsyth? It's Sir Harry Mortimer. I need a quick chat with you. Forsyth?"

No answer from within. Harry sensed Forsyth was still in there. But if the publisher didn't want to talk, Harry knew he was going to have to wait.

He turned and went back down the landing.

At the foot of the staircase, however, he stopped, hearing loud voices from below stairs.

McLeod's voice in particular. The man's Scottish brogue was like the deep rumbling of a rockfall in the highlands.

None too happy.

Harry was always reluctant to step in when there was a problem with the staff; Mydworth Manor, though officially his by inheritance, was Aunt Lavinia's domain.

But on a day like this, when, well, who knew what was happening, he felt it was perhaps his duty.

He turned and headed quickly down the narrow staircase that led to the kitchens, hearing the voices getting louder, a full-on argument in progress…

At the door to the kitchens, he stopped. Benton and Mrs Woodfine the housekeeper were attempting to restrain McLeod, as the cook raged and spluttered at the kitchen staff, most of whom seemed to be cowering in a corner.

On the stoves behind him, pans were bubbling – lunch clearly in mid-preparation – but all cooking activity appeared to have stopped.

"I say," said Harry, in the calmest voice he could summon. He saw the trio stop instantly – McLeod's mouth still half-open, mid-curse. "Anything I can do to help?"

KAT WAS SITTING ALONE in the library when she saw Harry go past down the main corridor.

"Harry, darling," she called – and his smiling face reappeared at the door.

"Aha!" he said, entering and shutting the door behind him. "How lovely and peaceful."

He came over, gave her a kiss on the cheek and then flopped in the armchair next to hers.

"Tough time ransacking Mr Carmody's room?" said Kat.

"Actually, I've just gone two rounds with McLeod and Mrs Woodfine in the kitchen."

"Ouch."

"Indeed. Seems one of the young staff, hired for the party, just ran for the hills last night, not to be seen again. Leaving McLeod's oysters unshucked."

"Interesting."

She saw him lean forward, face more serious.

"Isn't it? Curious thing is – I came across the lad myself last night. Nervous as hell, carrying a clasp knife around."

"In the kitchen?" said Kat, surprised. "For shucking?"

"Not that kind of knife. Apparently usually works on the fishing boats. That's why Mrs Woodfine hired him, shucker extraordinaire. But that knife… Been at the back of my mind."

"What time did he disappear?" said Kat.

"Last seen around midnight."

"After Carmody died."

"Exactly."

"You thinking – somehow – he's a possible suspect?"

"Don't know," said Harry. "But it's yet another odd thing from last night that doesn't quite smell right."

"That list is getting rather long. What's the boy's name?"

"Todd."

"He local?"

"Littlehampton. About half an hour away."

"We should talk to him."

"I agree," said Harry. "In the meantime, look what I found in Carmody's room…"

He removed an envelope from his jacket pocket, took out a note and handed it over. She read it, handed it back, then listened as Harry recounted his search and his meeting with Palmer.

"So, it was actually Palmer who found this note – and he handed it to you?" said Kat.

"He did," said Harry. "Why? Is that important?"

Kat now told him about her chat with the Sawyers – and with Quiller.

"Gosh," said Harry. "So Quiller says he saw *Palmer* go down to the lake?"

"Apparently. Though I know I saw Palmer in the house when we finished dancing. Remember? Playing billiards."

"That's right. It's possible he'd been down at the lake – then quickly slipped back into the house."

She saw Harry shake his head at that.

Right, she thought, *doesn't seem possible.*

"Easy enough to find out," Kat said. "Talk to the people he was playing with."

"Still doesn't make any sense though, does it?" said Harry. "If Palmer went down to the grotto intending to do Carmody harm, why show me the note? If he'd written it, he could have just pocketed it – I wouldn't have noticed."

"Could be a clever double bluff?" said Kat. "After all, he must have known you'd find it in the book eventually. And he may have even come to the room to hunt for it himself. Then, what better way to look innocent—"

"Than to find it, and give to me? Could be. And last night down at the lake, he certainly kept it quiet that he was there earlier."

"He's not the only one not telling all. I think Celine knows a lot more than she's revealed. She looked pretty nervous when she saw me talking to Quiller. Seems everybody's lying."

"But here's the thing, Lady Mortimer – which I am sure you have already taken note of – nobody's got a clear motive."

"Well, Forsyth obviously thinks Palmer *does*. But we're not going to know why until we talk to him," said Kat. "And that's not going to be anytime soon."

"Not until after lunch, I suspect," said Harry. "Which suits me down to the ground. I'm actually rather peckish. You?"

Kat laughed. "You mean hungry? Absolutely. And don't forget – I've got a tennis match to play this afternoon."

She watched him get up. "Come on then. Oysters or no – there is at least some jolly nice tomato bisque to be had."

"Already had a taste, hmm?"

"Down in the kitchen – couldn't resist."

She followed him out of the library to the dining room, where she could see the weekend guests already beginning to assemble.

So many questions…

What was Carmody up to?

Was he really murdered?

And, if so, who did it?

10.

MURDER INDEED

HARRY SIPPED HIS SOUP and looked around the lunch table. Still around thirty guests staying; some of whom he knew of old.

But his focus – on just a few.

Palmer who chatted politely with Lavinia at the head of the table.

Then Celine, charming, chattering away at the far end, a pair of generals laughing at every little joke she made.

Sawyer, only a few seats away from her, slurping soup automatically, head slightly bowed, ignored by the guests on either side.

And finally, Forsyth, who had appeared late, taking the last available seat, next to Quiller.

The newspaper magnate was no longer holding forth as he had at the party. Instead he toyed with his plate, muttering under his breath to Quiller, both men clearly taking care not to be overheard.

Harry caught Forsyth's eye and nodded. The man nodded back.

Key to everything would be what Forsyth had to say. With Quiller silent, only Forsyth might know just what Carmody had been up to. And why Palmer had cause to kill him.

Harry looked down the table to where Kat sat chatting to one of Lavinia's artist friends.

To a casual observer, thought Harry, *just a typical country house lunch.*

Who'd guess that perhaps one of these innocent-looking guests was a murderer?

"Excuse me, sir," came Benton's quiet voice in his ear.

Harry turned, to see the man leaning in confidentially.

"A telephone call for you, sir. *Dr Bedell.*"

"Thank you, Benton," said Harry, getting up, with a nod of apology to the table for the interruption, then heading out into the main hall where the telephone stood on a small table.

He checked up and down the corridor to ensure he wasn't being overheard, then picked up the phone.

"Mortimer here," he said. "Dr Bedell?"

"Sir Harry, not an inopportune time, I hope?"

"Not at all. You have something?"

"I do. Just got back from Chichester morgue, where they let me have a look at Carmody. Thought I should ring you straight away."

"You found something?"

"I did indeed," said the doctor. "Bruising on the neck and arms, indicative of a struggle immediately ante mortem."

"Couldn't have been caused by the fall?"

"No, I've seen contusions like these many times before, Sir Harry. Signs of a tight grip, arm round a neck etc. Somebody pretty damned determined. Attacked the poor chap from behind, I suspect."

"No hint of a cause of death though?"

"Not yet."

"If there was a struggle – could *that* have caused a heart attack?"

"Possibly. Depends on how long that struggle went on for. But there is something else I should tell you – though we'll have to wait for a full post-mortem to be sure."

"Go on."

"Spotted a very odd mark on the neck, Sir Harry. Some kind of... wound."

"Knife wound?" said Harry, thinking immediately of the young kitchen assistant.

"No, not a knife. Very small, near dots. Couple of puncture marks – almost like a bite of some kind. Then purplish bruising around the wound, and signs of some bleeding. To be honest – not seen anything like it before. At least on a cadaver."

"When's the post-mortem?"

"First thing tomorrow."

"Jolly good," said Harry. "Let me know as soon as you hear anything."

"I will. Rum thing, this, don't you know."

"It is indeed," said Harry. "Thanks for phoning."

"Bye then."

Harry put the receiver back on the stand and paused, before going back to the dining room to finish his soup.

There didn't seem much doubt about it now. Carmody had been murdered.

But how? And that all important question... who?

KAT WALKED WITH HARRY past the croquet lawn on the west side of Mydworth Manor towards the small copse of trees which she knew sheltered the tennis court.

She had her racquet in one hand, and a bag with her tennis clothes slung over one shoulder.

She'd not played tennis for months, and hoped she wouldn't be too rusty. Over the years, in various diplomatic postings she'd been a regular player, making plenty of friends through the game.

Right now, though, she wasn't thinking about tennis – she was thinking about Carmody.

"Puncture marks?" she said, as they followed the path together into the trees.

"Yep," said Harry. "Strange, no?"

"My first thought – well, it's almost too crazy to say it…"

"Snake?"

"Yes!" said Kat. "Can be a classic tool of assassination."

"I know! Turks lost one of their agents that way in Istanbul. But here in Sussex? Yes, it is crazy."

"Guess we'll just have to wait for the post-mortem. Meanwhile, I've got a doubles game to play. Kinda looking forward to it."

"Me too," said Harry as they emerged from the trees into the most idyllic scene. Kat looked around and took in the setting: a perfect grass court surrounded by tall hedges.

At one end, a green painted changing hut; at the other, a small pavilion with tables set out for teas.

A foursome was already playing, the game looking to Kat like a light-hearted knockabout.

Celine was already waiting with her racquet and bag. The singer came over, smiled at Harry, nodded to Kat.

"Who are we playing?" said Kat, looking around for the other doubles pair.

"Change of plan," said Celine. "Singles now."

"Oh," said Kat. "Just me and you?"

"Yes." Then, with a bit of an edge, "That okay Lady Mortimer?"

Kat shrugged, not sure about Celine's brisk tone. "Sure."

"Your dear husband not joining us to watch the combat?" said Harry, looking around the small crowd of guests.

"He's… indisposed," said Celine. "In our room, I believe."

One word for it, thought Kat. *At lunch he looked positively pie-eyed.*

"We should get changed," said Celine.

Kat watched her walk by the side of the court towards the changing cabin.

"CHARMING," SAID KAT to Harry.

"Nerves?" said Harry.

"I thought you said these games were just a bit of *fun?*" said Kat.

"Usually," said Harry. "Just play nicely now, won't you?"

"I always do."

"Think I've got the scars to prove otherwise."

"You going to watch?"

"Absolutely. I'll be the one eating scones and jam and cheering."

"For me, I hope."

"Of course. The honour of the Mortimers is at stake."

"Save me a piece of fruit cake," said Kat, and she headed over to the changing hut where Celine was waiting.

THE CHANGING CABIN, Kat thought, was surprisingly primitive in comparison to places she'd played back home in New York.

As a girl, she would take the IRT Subway to the Fordham College courts, racquet in its press, feeling more than self-conscious on a crowded subway.

To find a whole suite of dressing rooms, complete with showers.

But England was a different world. And so unpredictable.

Kat looked over at Celine Dubois as she laced up her tennis shoes.

Though Kat felt that she herself pulled off the tennis whites in better-than-good fashion, Celine – well – she looked like *something else.*

She looks fantastic, Kat thought. *But I wonder if she can play tennis?* She'd soon find out.

So far there had not been any chit-chat between the two, the atmosphere having turned icy. Kat wondered if the conversation she'd had this morning with Quiller may have put Celine on the defensive.

Did the singer suspect that Kat now knew all about her affair with Palmer?

That would make anyone upset.

"I was wondering…"

Celine, racquet held firmly in hand, stood up.

"Yes?"

Yeah, definite coolness there.

Too bad. Kat knew that Celine and Lavinia had – at one time – been close. As Kat now knew, that was before her great success as a singer, and the marriage to a movie star.

"The rules, I mean, American tennis, English tennis, are they—?"

Celine took some steps towards her.

"Did you just say 'American' tennis?" Then – a dismissive laugh. "Your people think they invented *everything*, don't they? Suppose you created golf too? Be sure you don't tell McLeod."

Though there was an edge here, Kat kept a smile on her face.

"No, I just meant… are the rules a bit different?"

Celine took a moment to respond.

"The rules, Lady Mortimer, are precisely the same, and the skills required, no different."

Kat nodded, while Celine said, with a nod to the door that led out of the tiny dressing cabin, "Shall we?"

Kat stood up, grabbing her racquet from the wooden bench, thinking, *I just may have a real game ahead of me here.*

11.

ANYONE FOR TENNIS

HARRY STOOD AT ONE end of the court, finally alone.

It seemed that so many of the guests, many who had not seen him in years, wanted to come up, have a few innocuous welcoming words.

Harry – of course – responded gracefully.

It's not as if they would suspect that Carmody's death was any more than a heart attack?

As he waited for Kat to come out for the next match, Harry scanned the little groups of spectators, some holding tea cups and saucers, looking about as English as one can.

Others took the flute glasses being passed on silver trays. Benton was back to overseeing his troops, not helping out with canapés.

As one of the maids passed by, Harry looked at a glass.

"I say, what do we have here?"

The glass of something bubbly sent its steady stream to the surface, but also had a red object at the base as if it was generating the carbonation.

"Sir, champagne with a spot of brandy and bitters, and a maraschino cherry at the bottom."

The girl's accent... *Pretty thick*, thought Harry. *Yorkshire perhaps?*

"Well, wonders will never cease. English innovation at its finest."

"Would you care for one, sir?"

"Tad early in the day for me, but thank you. Tea and some scones would be just lovely, though."

The young server, keeping the tray perfectly balanced, curtsied, and then moved on.

Which is when he saw Palmer. Leaning against the side of the pavilion. Alone, with neither a cup of fortifying tea or the bubbly concoction.

And Harry thought, *Not too sure what he made of my searching Carmody's room.*

The note sent to Carmody, folded in Harry's jacket pocket, felt like an incendiary device.

And in a way it is, he thought.

It meant someone had *lured* Carmody to the grotto last night. And, given what Dr Bedell had said, that meant Carmody almost certainly had been murdered.

Eventually, Harry would need to talk to Palmer again.

But for now, that had better wait. Harry had learned, especially working with the ever-strategic Kat, that timing is nearly the whole ball of wax.

Ball of wax... one of her sayings.

Wherever do Americans get these expressions from? he thought.

Which is when two stunning women in near matching and brilliant tennis whites, came out onto the court.

One of them, his wife Kat.

KAT POSITIONED HERSELF TOWARDS the back, knees slightly bent, racquet up.

She turned and looked right to see a young man on a high chair, presiding over the net. Lavinia had installed one of her footmen as an umpire. So much for the casual game of tennis that had been promised the day before…

"Just a little knockabout, to clear the cobwebs away," Lavinia had said.

But Kat had been around the English long enough to know that though on the surface a sport might be "just a game", in practice it was anything but.

And certainly, Celine didn't appear to be in any kind of playful mood.

That referee might well turn out to be helpful, she thought, considering how many arguments she had gotten into as a young girl.

Was a ball in or out?

Many a heated debate she had had on *that* weighty question.

Facing her, Celine bounced the tennis ball, once, twice, as if testing its mettle, getting ready to serve.

The service was always so revealing of what kind of match lay ahead.

Another bounce, then the ball tossed into the air, and Celine's racquet came back hard and flew in a fierce arc; straight, with a slight angle down, as the tennis ball rocketed at Kat.

FROM THE DECK OF the pavilion, Harry watched Kat race to the left to return Celine's service.

And while Kat was strong – a great tennis player in Harry's opinion, she always beat him – she now had to scramble to return the ball.

Kat's shot wasn't much of a threat to Celine and the French woman won the first point easily.

MURDER WORE A MASK

Harry took a sip of tea, then smeared a scone with cream and jam, took a bite – and settled back to watch.

Back and forth the first game went, the rallies getting longer, as slowly Kat got her "legs", found a bit more control.

Harry and the other spectators clapped the points politely, as more guests began to drift towards the court, attracted by the sound of a real game in progress.

And no doubt about it, thought Harry. *This* is *a real game. Celine Dubois isn't going to take prisoners here.*

Kat's turn to serve.

Harry knew to his own cost how hard she could power these down. Not for her the genteel underarm serves that some of the Embassy wives used to deploy back in Cairo.

Her first serve clipped the line, kicking up chalk and flying past Celine before she could even prepare a shot.

Harry saw the singer pause, staring at Kat, eyes narrowing.

Uh-oh, he thought. *Snake's been prodded with a stick.*

He watched as Kat served again. This time Celine was ready for it – smashing her return across the net and straight into Kat's stomach.

A collective "oooh" rang around the court from the spectators.

Harry saw Kat gasp and bend double in pain, then crouch.

"*Terribly* sorry," said Celine, approaching the net and – to Harry's eye at least – putting on a good pretence at concern. "Awful accident. You okay?"

Doesn't look that sorry, thought Harry, wondering if he should go to Kat's assistance.

But he knew his wife wouldn't appreciate that. He watched as – true to form – Kat stood up, brushed the mark of the ball from her top – and smiled at her opponent.

"Not to worry," said Kat. "Your point. Good shot, Celine."

He saw Kat smile at him before returning to the back line to serve again. But he knew from the steely look in her eyes that she wouldn't give up now until Celine was beaten.

No doubt about it, this had been – up until now – Celine's show.

But Harry was pretty sure it wouldn't stay that way.

And when Celine lost the game and the umpire rather nervously called out, one game all, Harry thought *this is turning into quite a match.*

COME ON, KAT SAID to herself, twenty minutes later. *You're better than this.*

But Kat had to admit that Celine was not only an amazing singer, she moved on this court like a *pro.*

Every game had been hard-fought, the ball zinging across the net. Kat wondered whether the sedate surroundings of Mydworth Manor had ever seen such a women's match.

Nonetheless, she felt she had finally found her footing.

And she knew that her backhand, always troublesome for some players, was her secret weapon. Strong, fast – that backhand shot always went exactly where she wanted.

So, settling into a rhythm of returns, Kat took the points and heard "five games all". The score finally tied.

Now – it was anyone's game.

BUT THEN, AS KAT prepared to receive serve again, Harry spotted some late arrivals, to the right, midcourt.

Horatio Forsyth and, walking with him, Gerald Quiller.

Timing, Harry thought again. *Questions to be asked and all that.*

At last, the chance to talk to the man who was so sure that Carmody had been murdered – and who feared he might be next.

Harry got up from his table by the pavilion and walked around the court to where Forsyth and Quiller now stood.

"Mr Forsyth," said Harry, approaching.

Harry saw the publisher look over, his eyes rheumy. Maybe a tough night? Quiller turned and looked as well, his eyes actually beady, the man's pivot, slow and precise like the sluggish beam from an ancient light house.

Or like a hungry owl, Harry thought.

"Sir Harry, er, umm, good day."

Harry smiled and gave a nod to Quiller.

"I was wondering, Mr Forsyth, if we might have a private word?"

Forsyth shook his head, almost angrily. "I'm happy for Quiller to hear *whatever* we talk about. But not here. Somewhere a little more discreet, if you don't mind."

Harry looked over at the match. The umpire pronouncing "deuce", the game tied, with the last points up for grabs.

"I know just the place. If you'd just wait a moment. Seems my wife is about to win… or lose. Don't want to miss that either way."

KAT HAD TO DO an awkward lunge at Celine's service, which well into the match, remained strong, precise.

But though some of Kat's returns had become a bit wobbly, her powerful backhand now sent the ball flying over the highest part of the net.

She saw Celine, now the one scrambling to the side, diving and just returning the drive.

The ball landed on the line right at Kat's feet.

Back in the Bronx, a vociferous debate would have ensued.

But here?

"Out," the referee said. And Celine – though clearly disagreeing with the call – nodded politely and returned to her position.

Kat could feel Celine's distraction as the French woman tossed the ball in the air to serve again.

One needed to manage emotions in a tennis game, and this time, Kat's return flew into a corner, just "in", with Celine unable to get near it.

"Game, set and match," said the umpire quickly.

Celine stopped. Game over.

In a full match, it would be the best of three sets. But this, well – as Lavinia had promised – was just a "casual game", other players ready to jump in.

Celine's face, not happy.

Apparently not such a good loser, Kat thought. *Must remember that.*

The little groups sitting at nearby tables, and others standing by the sidelines of the court, clapped.

Kat hurried to the net.

"Great game," she said, extending a hand.

Celine had walked over slowly. Face still set.

Then, begrudgingly, "Well played, Lady Mortimer."

"You as well! How about we get changed and grab one of those lovely flutes everyone seems to have?"

At that, a tight smile.

"Yes, absolutely."

They both turned and walked off their respective sides of the court.

But not before Kat saw Harry, the publisher and his writer, walking away.

He must have seen me win, she thought.

MURDER WORE A MASK

Normally, Harry would be there, cheering the loudest, running over, giving her one of his great, exuberant hugs.

But instead he was heading somewhere with those two; Forsyth finally in their firing line.

And that was fine because, trailing Celine, now heading back to the little dressing room, *Kat had plans as well.*

12.

THE TRUTH ABOUT MR CARMODY

HARRY OPENED THE DOOR to Lavinia's greenhouse, the always remarkable collection of scents and aromas hitting him immediately.

Amazon lilies, Chinese hibiscus, African violets – and the venerable English rose.

A nervous-looking Forsyth, accompanied by the raptor-like Quiller followed behind.

And over at the other end – with plants awaiting potting, pots and trowels at the ready - Mr Grayer, Lavinia's long-time gardener. He turned, looking.

"Sir Harry," Grayer said, surprised perhaps to have sudden guests while he was in the middle of re-potting.

"Mr Grayer, I wonder if you could, um, leave us for a moment? Little chat we need to have."

Grayer immediately put down a pot, and with a nod and smile said, "Certainly. Plants outside need some tending to anyway, after last night's 'festivities'."

Harry grinned back. "I'm sure."

And as soon as the gardener left, he turned to Forsyth.

"Okay. Mr Forsyth, I doubt anyone will stumble upon us here. And as you're okay with Mr Quiller here listening, shall we talk?"

And at that, Forsyth not only nodded - but gulped.

FRESH OUT OF THE primitive dressing room shower, the water ice-cold, tired old towels piled beside each locker, Kat felt that Celine was doing her best to say absolutely *nothing*.

Feeling chagrined at the loss?

Or – something else entirely?

Kat wanted to know about Palmer. But she felt she needed to get a conversation going here, something to unfreeze the atmosphere.

She started chatting as they dressed, both of them opting for slacks and crisp tailored shirts, Celine's a robin's egg blue, Kat's a pale green.

"I love your blouse," Kat said, then felt straight away that this initial attempt at making chit-chat sounded terribly odd.

Not surprisingly, in reply she got a perfunctory, "Thanks."

Okay, Kat thought. *Time for a more direct route.*

She slipped on her shoes, stylish two-tone brown and beige pumps. And noticing such things, as one does, she saw Celine put on her jet-black pumps as well.

"Celine, this morning. When we talked…" That at least got the woman's attention as she turned and looked, but said nothing. "I had the distinct feeling that there was something more you wanted to say?"

Flatly: "No, I didn't."

Kat smiled at that and stood up. She took a small step closer to Celine. This tall woman was quite obviously – from the robust match they just played – as much muscle and strength as grace and beauty.

"You see, I found it odd your husband did not *remember* meeting Mr Palmer. When he was indisposed on the ship."

Celine looked away at that, perhaps considering if she might simply walk away. Out of the dressing room, and out of range of Kat's suddenly probing questions.

Kat certainly hoped not. This set-up – the two of them, alone – had been hard-won.

"My husband," Celine finally said, "is *often* indisposed. Especially these days. Has trouble remembering lots of things."

Kat nodded at that.

But she wasn't buying it at all.

In his cups or not, someone like Sawyer, an actor, would be attentive to people, remembering meeting them, sizing them up.

And Palmer, brash and so full of himself, would not be so easy to forget.

"I see. But there is something else I was curious about."

"Curious? You know what that did to the cat."

Ouch, thought Kat. Celine's eyes were focused on her, perhaps sensing that there was some dangerous probing being done here, and now pushing back.

Undeterred, Kat pressed on.

"One question that, well, since talking to Fleet Street's finest this morning, I *really* need to ask you."

And as if they were back on the clay courts, Celine waited…

"MR FORSYTH, YOU KNOW, of course, that my Aunt Lavinia came to see me and my wife about the Carmody matter. About your concerns."

Harry looked from Forsyth to Quiller; one a roly-poly man, with florid face; the other, looking like he hadn't been fed for weeks, ready to swoop down on any morsel of food - or information.

"Yes. I didn't tell her everything. Quite frankly, she didn't want to know."

"Right. Something about how after Carmody's unfortunate, well, whatever it was, you felt *you* might be next?"

A nod.

"*Next*. That would imply murder. Intent."

Another nod.

Small curves at the side of Quiller's mouth suggested he was enjoying this line of questioning.

Harry shot him a quick look, as if to say, *I might have a few questions for you too, Mr Quiller.*

"Yes," Forsyth said. "I suppose, if you are to help me, you'd best know the truth."

"That's usually how it works."

"You see, Mr Carmody and I had an 'arrangement'."

"Arrangement?"

Forsyth looked at Quiller. Harry guessed that whenever one was spilling the beans, one always checked with associates and accomplices before said beans got spilled.

"A *deal*. Carmody had agreed to reveal everything he knew about his boss, Mr Palmer. The works. Every scandal. Every secret, dirty deal that Palmer did to enrich himself at the public's expense. Every nasty liaison. *All of it.*"

"For money?"

Forsyth's head bobbed again as Harry turned to Quiller. "And you, Mr Quiller were due to write the article, this series of exposés?"

Finally, the silent partner spoke.

"Why, yes I was. Just waiting for the documents to be given to me. The information, you see. Evidence."

"What kind of evidence? Affairs you mean?"

"Not *just* affairs," said Quiller. And then, actually licking his lips: "There's a child. Or as Mr Forsyth's headline writers prefer to call it 'a secret love child'."

"Outside his marriage? But that would destroy him."

"Exactly."

Harry had spent a good amount of time around writers.

Some were great fun to be with, living by their wits, always knowing the best watering holes, and with an appetite for life that belied their profession of sitting down and hammering out words.

Others, though, had the behaviour and demeanour of monks awaiting the next *auto-da-fé*.

Quiller clearly belonged to the latter crowd.

"You mentioned documents, Mr Forsyth. Did you get them?"

"*No.* You see, the first batch, to accompany my initial substantial payments to him, was to be handed over this very weekend."

Harry thought back to his rifling through Carmody's briefcase, finding absolutely nothing of interest.

Did Carmody neglect to bring them? Had something gone wrong with his "deal" with Forsyth?

Did he perhaps mean to call the whole thing off?

Well, that wouldn't have been good for Forsyth's newspapers. And the same, Harry suddenly thought, for Mr Quiller.

Harry took a breath.

He had one last question.

"Forsyth – let me be as clear with you as I can. If you are right, and Mr Carmody was murdered…" Forsyth nodded in agreement, looking the part of someone in danger. "Do you know who that killer might be?"

Forsyth took a deep breath, puffy chest swelling even further. And to that question, he most definitely did have an answer.

CELINE HAD ALSO TAKEN a step closer.

Even though Kat knew that the two of them were quite alone here, the closeness, the lowered voices, indicated that Celine wanted this conversation to remain strictly between the two of them.

"Go on," she said flatly to Kat, eyes locked on.

"You said you danced at the various ship events with Mr Palmer?"

"He was most accommodating."

"I bet," Kat said. Celine's eyes turned steely. "When you returned to London, did you continue seeing him? Albeit, perhaps not for dancing. Maybe – other activities?"

And Kat felt as if she had poured kerosene on a smouldering fire... and yet... there was delay.

Before the flames erupted.

"You know," said Celine. "I do so *love* American music. Cole Porter. Gershwin. Duke Ellington. Nothing like it being written anywhere else, I can tell you."

"And you sing it beaut—"

Celine cut her off. "But the American *people?* Something about them that's all a little hard to stomach."

Kat let the insult land.

Not the first time she had been with someone compelled to deliver an opinion about her fellow citizens from the New World.

She paused a moment.

"You didn't answer the question, Celine. Are you having an affair with Palmer?"

And then Kat saw something else in those dark and beautiful eyes.

Concern – and a smidge of worry.

"My private life, Lady Mortimer, is precisely that. Private."

"True – for now. But I suspect Cyril Palmer's private life is about to get very public. And yours with it."

"What do you mean?"

Kat paused for a second. *Should she reveal what she and Harry suspected? What if Celine was involved too?*

It was a risky call – but she felt she had no choice.

"Celine – it's almost certain that Wilfred Carmody was murdered last night."

"Really?" said Celine, her voice betraying no emotion – or even interest.

"It's also possible that Cyril Palmer may have been involved in the crime."

Kat watched Celine carefully, but the singer's face was motionless.

"How ridiculous."

"You don't know anything about this?"

"Of *course* not. It's like something out of one of your trashy dime novels."

"Ridiculous or not, the police are likely to be involved soon. And your movements last night? They will be investigated."

"Are you threatening me?"

"Warning you."

Kat stood her ground as Celine stepped close.

"They said Sir Harry had married beneath himself," said Celine, her face close. "I see now – they were right."

And at that, Celine turned and walked out.

Good riddance, thought Kat.

After waiting a few seconds, gathering her thoughts and suspicions, Kat left the dressing room as well.

Eager to find Harry, and catch up.

What a weekend this is turning out to be, Kat thought.

What else could be ahead?

13.

A QUIET MOMENT

KAT WATCHED HARRY – his crisp white shirt with sleeves rolled up – pulling on the two oars of a bright red rowboat.

Those arms, already tanned from the warm and – so far – sunny summer.

No one else was out in the water, most hurrying into the manor house for a sure-to-be lavish afternoon tea put out by Lavinia's staff.

As to the early evening, there'd be an array of activities for guests to choose from: from a ride through the nearby trail, to some skeet shooting overseen by Mr Grayer down near the open meadow.

More and more, Lavinia had told Kat, she had gone off the idea of "hunting".

Far better if people just blow up clay pigeons, Lavinia had said. *No harm, no foul – literally.*

Though Kat knew that, in her day, Lavinia had had a reputation as an excellent shot, not adverse to the hunt.

Now she watched Harry, sweat on his brow, do the yeoman's job of ploughing through the water.

She was curious about the conversation they were about to have, discoveries shared, and then *plans.*

They were nearly mid-lake, sun glistening on the water; sparkling, jewel-like dots that flashed on the surface and then vanished as the water rippled and eddied.

"So – think we're quite out of earshot?"

At that, Harry laughed. "Ha. You see, I always think it's better to hide in plain sight. If we had gone off somewhere, two of us, walking on our own…"

"Any guilty parties would get suspicious?"

"Precisely. And so far, knock—" Harry tapped the wood near one of the oar locks "—on wood, no one among the guests has come up with a sudden pressing reason to return to London."

"Which itself would be quite suspicious."

"Oh yes. But then, with what little we can prove – I mean, once we've had our chat out here – there's no way to stop anyone from actually leaving. And questioning them, when they are safely ensconced back in Mayfair or wherever."

"Would be difficult. Yes. So, us out here – meant to look like a romantic *bateau à deux* for the relatively new newlyweds."

"You know, I rather like the sound of that. I should have wrangled a bottle of Perrier-Jouët from Benton, maybe a wedge of the camembert and some bread? Have you tasted McLeod's bread by the way? I have no idea where the man gets his yeast, but it's something."

Kat looked back at the manor house. "Lavinia won't miss us?"

"I imagine she'll think we are doing what we can to resolve the fate of Mr Carmody."

Kat smiled, their "game" about to begin. This was always fun. "Me first?"

"Oh yes. And by the way, did I tell you how smashing you were on the court? Quite a display."

"Yes. And even more interesting was the conversation I had with my opponent when we changed."

"All ears, as they say…"

And Kat began.

"SO SHE WAS HIDING something?" asked Harry.

"Most definitely. I mean, as much as one can trust instincts. Powerful man like Palmer? Might be some women's type."

"Not yours?"

Kat grinned. "No, Sir Harry. I know my type. Looking right at him."

"Oh, that's good. Jolly reassuring. And what else do you think she was hiding?"

"That's just it. When I mentioned Carmody – and Palmer's possible involvement – she turned very nasty. But you know, Harry, it felt like bluster. Like she knew something but was feeling cornered."

"Speaking of secrets – let's not forget her husband this morning. You think he really forgot about meeting Palmer and Carmody?"

"Again unlikely."

Harry looked away, wondering how these suspicions connected to what he had just learned from Forsyth.

"Damned curious that. But – if what we've heard is correct – the singer and the MP are still continuing their dalliance. Both hiding something, for different reasons. Tad perplexing all that."

"Just a tad," Kat said, laughing. "Okay. Your turn."

"Right, then."

He told her about the deal Forsyth had with Carmody. The evidence of corruption. But also… of an illegitimate child.

"Now here's the interesting part, Kat. The child was born fifteen years ago when Palmer first became an MP, living in Chichester. Palmer was already married – and apparently he was pretty ruthless dealing with the problem."

"Doesn't surprise me."

"According to Forsyth, Palmer had the girl fired from her job in service. Pretty much put her out on the streets. Then the child was taken away from her."

"God. Then what happened to the mother?"

Harry shook his head. "Died just a year later."

"How awful."

"Par for the course with men like that, sadly."

"And what about the kid?"

"According to Forsyth, the child – a boy – only recently discovered the identity of his father. Tried to make contact."

"Let me guess – Palmer told him where to get off?"

"Precisely. Threatened him, the works."

"And Carmody had evidence of all this?"

"Letters, affidavits, diary notes. The lot."

"Sounds like motive to me."

"Me too. But here's where it gets interesting. The boy wrote to Palmer, told him if he didn't acknowledge him as his son he'd kill him."

"Wow. When was this?"

"Just weeks ago. And there's something even more interesting."

"Tell me."

"The boy's name: Todd. Charlie Todd."

"Wait – that's the lad in the kitchen – the one who disappeared!"

"Exactly," said Harry.

"He must have known Palmer was going to be here last night! Hey – maybe he went after him, down to the grotto?"

"That's what I was thinking."

"In which case, he may have seen something. Something that made him run. Harry, we have to find him! Do you know where he lives?"

"I do – got an address from Mrs Woodfine who hired him. Littlehampton."

"But that's just half an hour away."

"Indeed."

"Well, what are we waiting for?" said Kat.

"The tide, actually," said Harry, smiling. "Pound to a penny Todd's out on a fishing boat today. And the fleet won't be back in until seven, earliest. Until then, nothing we can do."

KAT LET HER FINGERS slip into the cool lake water, dangling, as she listened. The whole setting here peaceful and serene.

"Something that worries me, Harry."

"Go on."

"We're so certain it's Palmer that did it. But quite *how* – well, we don't know, right? And though we've got motive now – do we have means? And opportunity?"

"The classic trio! And true!"

"How about this: what if Forsyth and Quiller are making this up? What if they're behind it?"

"Well, that wins the 'interesting' prize. Forsyth – he's genuinely scared. And he and Carmody together were in - your word – cahoots? To destroy Palmer. So, amazingly, it makes sense."

"But only if Palmer knew."

"Ah, there you go. You're right. We don't know that yet."

"There is another question, Harry."

"Which is?"

"Even if Palmer *did* know that his loyal aide was about to betray him, reveal all that dirty laundry…"

"Yes, go on."

Kat pulled her hand out of the water. Brushed it across her brow – the water on her skin delightfully cool.

"Would that be enough for Palmer to murder Carmody? Risk everything?"

"Oh, I don't know. Your whole life shamed? Political plans crushed? Seems like a pretty good motive to me."

"No doubt. But then the question – *how* did he do it? And, if he did, how did he get back to the house so quickly?"

"One of a plethora of questions we have."

"You know, when we went down to Carmody, by the lake?"

"Yes?" Harry said.

"Did you notice anything odd? At the time, maybe not seeming relevant?"

"Dead man, in costume, weird mask and… ah, hang on. Mask."

Kat smiled. "Right. His costume, Harry. I didn't see a mask. Did you?"

"You're right. Isn't that interesting? Didn't really register at the time."

Kat laughed. "However, just as I thought we were getting close to the solution, that confuses things."

"Sometimes confusion can be quite useful."

And Kat grinned. "If you say so, Harry. It does give us a good reason to have another chat with Palmer."

"Indeed."

Kat looked away, thinking, *there still* has *to be more going on here that we don't know.*

"I'll row us back."

"Nope. My turn," Kat said.

"Absolutely."

And then they both stood up in the small boat, which did a funny wobble, as they slid past each other.

A sweet moment, Kat thought.

Changing places, brushing by each other.

She grabbed the oars, their ends smooth with the patina of years of people grabbing them tight.

Harry's eyes, catching full sunlight now, always piercing.

Kat started rowing.

"One more thing, Lady Mortimer."

Kat had found a good rhythm – the oars rising from the water, then cutting into the lake again – the boat moving steadily back to the shore, and Lavinia's small boathouse.

"Yes?"

"This whole thing – dangerous for Forsyth. And maybe dangerous for anyone trying to get to the bottom of things."

"Yes. Best we take care. We want to solve this mystery, not become part of it."

And Harry, bright sun on his face, nodded seriously as he lay back against the bow and Kat rowed them back.

14.

A TRIP TO THE SEA

"HARRY – THIS IS *absolutely* beautiful."

Kat watched as Harry navigated the winding road, much too narrow in her opinion for vehicles moving in *both* directions. But her husband – behind the wheel of their Alvis – seemed unfazed.

Even when they had to pass a farmer's truck that seemed to be barrelling right at them.

"This – ah yes – the Sussex Downs. The rolling hills, the perfect stands of trees, as if someone arranged it all."

"Haven't seen anything like it, especially now, sun setting."

Harry turned to her.

Something she wished he *wouldn't* do while driving. Despite her own comfort behind the wheel almost anywhere, here she'd much prefer his eyes straight ahead.

"Whenever I used to think of home, fond thoughts from abroad and all that, I'd think of just this place. To me, well… it *was* England."

Kat turned from Harry to look ahead as they entered a tunnel made by over-arching trees, encircling the road and the car.

Making it nearly as dark as night.

Harry flipped the lights on.

"These trees. They just *grow* this way?"

"Good question. One for Grayer? Always assumed they did. Does make it rather dark though, even in daytime!"

They emerged at the other end of the tree tunnel, to a small rise, and then…

"The sea, Harry!"

"*Knew* we were heading in the right direction."

Again, he turned to her. "Ready for a visit to the exciting fishing port of Littlehampton?"

HARRY HAD PARKED THE car in a space right near the beach. With the sun low in the west, the sand and shingle beach looked inviting, and some people, shoes off, were walking near the edge.

But Kat noticed – no one swimming.

"You know, Harry, when I was a kid my dad would take me to a beach called Riis Park. We'd stay till just about dusk. Swimming at that time… somehow the water felt… silky, magical in the orange light."

"Well, the only thing magical about the water here is that it's bloody cold. Not the Med, you know?"

But then she saw him looking out to sea and sensed a change in his mood.

"My parents would bring me here as a boy. When I was little, on the sand, I once tried to dig my way to China." He laughed. "So they said."

Kat laughed as well – but she still sensed something serious to come.

"One time though, they brought me to see the fishing boats, buy some fresh fish, right off the boat. My father could be like that. I was eleven I imagine… twelve."

Still Harry hadn't turned his eyes away from the sea.

"And he put a hand on my shoulder and said, 'Harry my boy, I think you're old enough for a big trip to see the Wonder City'."

"Wonder City?"

"Why, your very own New York, Kat. And shortly after that, he made plans, booked us on a transatlantic crossing."

He stopped.

And Kat remained silent because moments like this were important, fragile.

She knew that that trip was the last time he'd ever seen his parents.

Kat listened. Harry was not the crying type. He had some inner core that was too tough for that.

Outside of a deep breath – she could hear nothing.

Then he turned to her, took her hand.

"Shall we head over to the quay? Boats probably all back by now. Find our Charlie Todd?"

"Yes. Let's."

And as they walked together away from the beach, she noted that he had his confident smile back in place.

But in his blue eyes? A different story.

"THIS STRETCH, WHERE THE river comes down, always been here, but it's been made wider, more boats."

As they walked, Harry saw the fishing trawlers on both sides of the narrow harbour made by the river. Decks being washed down, the catch being dragged up from below decks. Soon trucks would show up, loaded with great blocks of ice.

But also, locals wandered by, eager to see what, for a bargain price, could be purchased fresh, and wrapped tight in newspaper – which did little to absorb the smell and slipperiness.

"Todd's boat, the one we're looking for… The Marie-Belle? Think that's probably it over there," he said pointing.

Kat nodded. In minutes they'd be beside the boat. But, as they walked, he felt her touch his arm.

"Harry. This man Todd. He had a knife. Remember?"

"Think he might turn nasty? In which case, we'd better stay out of reach of that first lunge, eh?"

Harry turned to her.

"I'll rely on your instincts here, Kat. Think you sense danger a lot quicker than I do."

She laughed. "And I think you may be better dealing with the after-effects once it rears its nasty head."

"Not so sure about that. Okay. Here we are. And there's Todd, if I'm not mistaken."

He gestured to where a young man in dark-green rubber fishing overalls stood on one of the decks, stacking crates.

The same young lad he'd seen the previous night in the kitchen at Mydworth Manor.

"You think he'll talk?" said Harry.

"Don't think he's got much choice. We can paint a pretty dark picture of what he was up to last night. Put him at the heart of it."

"Leverage?"

"Persuasion," said Kat as they reached the Marie-Belle. "Shall we?"

KAT SAW HARRY WAIT until Todd and his fellow workers put down their crates of fish. Other crewmen were already scrubbing the deck, something Kat guessed had to be done daily with so many fish being pulled aboard in big nets.

"I say, Todd. What was running today?"

At that, Charlie Todd looked up. His eyes instantly narrowed. A man with a pipe and lopsided cap, the image of a trawler captain, came over.

"Good run of cod, sir. Some nice Dover sole as well." The captain shot Todd a look as if curious how these two well-heeled people on the pier knew him. "Like some?"

Kat saw Harry scratch his head. Todd stood stock-still.

"Would indeed. Good size crate of both. Maybe have them loaded into the back of my car? The Alvis, down the quay there. But I wonder if we might have a quick word with your crewman here."

"Todd? The man still has a lot of work to do… just to go off, talking and all. Missed a whole day already and—"

Kat saw Harry pull out his wallet.

"Oh, I completely understand. Take this for the fish. And maybe a little extra, hmm?"

Todd had turned to the captain. Kat thought he had the look of someone who could – any minute – bolt. But right now, the choice was either jumping into the water, or trying to barrel past them.

"Don't mind. I'll talk to them," he said quietly.

Surprising, thought Kat.

And she waited with Harry as Todd peeled off his rubber overalls, stained with fish guts, and clambered out of the old trawler.

"Just a few minutes, you hear," the captain barked.

Kat was not at all sure that was how long it would be.

There were so many questions.

HARRY WATCHED AS THE fisherman, fists actually clenched, stood on the pier, looking from him, then to Kat, as if ready to "pop".

He saw Kat take a breath.

Such things didn't intimidate her.

"Charlie, why don't we take a little walk, down towards the beach? Away from the boats."

While that didn't seem to make the young fisherman relax, he did nod. And then the three of them began to walk away.

Harry looked over his shoulder, the grizzled old captain watching them, definitely wondering what the hell was going on.

"I imagine you want know the reason we're here?"

Charlie nodded again, "Bloody well do. Got my work to do, and you two? From your big house, coming here? *Why*?"

"Oh, the manor house – that's my aunt's. Our own place is not that big, not that big at all."

The attempt at humour did little to dissipate the tension.

"You see, Charlie," Kat began, her voice low, soothing.

Harry could well imagine that if he had a dark secret, such careful probing might get him to open up. Part of that was just who Kat was. But he knew she'd also picked up a few tricks during her time working with a law firm back in Manhattan. Not all of them pleasant.

"We *know* why you went to Mydworth Manor, and got that job in the kitchen."

Charlie turned like he was about to snarl at Kat.

"What you talking about? Just a spot of extra cash, is all it was. They needed—"

Kat looked away from him; no more was needed to cut off the false explanation.

"Right," said Kat, "guess most people *might* believe that story. If they didn't know the true one."

All the time, Harry had his eyes locked on the man.

A fisherman could be damned quick with a knife. And despite the fact they'd reached the far end of the harbour, Charlie Todd could still be feeling trapped and desperate.

"True story?" he said, spitting out the words. "What's that then?"

Another big breath from Kat, her timing – Harry thought – impeccable.

"That you went to the house because Cyril Palmer would be there. You went there because that man is your father, and he is responsible for your mother's death. Now isn't that right?"

At this, though they kept walking in unison, Harry felt an immediate grimness – despite the blue-sky day turning a wondrous purple, sun just going down, clouds picking up splotches of flaming red and orange.

A beautiful scene if they weren't discussing murder.

But Todd said nothing.

And Kat continued.

"You went there because you had decided to kill him."

And, at that, finally Charlie Todd stopped.

"HOW THE *HELL* d'you know anything like that? You two don't know me, don't know—"

Kat took a step closer to the man and – if anything – she made her voice lower.

Crucial moment here, she thought, if she wasn't to simply set the young man off.

"We know, Charlie. The reporter at the party? He knew all about your story, your plans, how you'd threatened Palmer. How Palmer ignored you. So – is that why you were at the house, Charlie? To murder him? 'Cept, you killed the wrong man?"

Charlie shook his head. "No. That's not what happened."

Harry cleared his throat.

Kat loved the way he sensed when it was time for him to enter the fray.

Because this definitely had the makings of a "fray".

"See now, Charlie, we have other evidence," he said. "We even have the note you sent. And yet somehow it ended up that poor Carmody was the one down by the grotto – the one you killed. By mistake, of course. But to a judge, murder is murder."

Charlie could not be shaking his head more violently.

Kat saw Harry turn, look around, as if giving Todd time to think.

To fabricate a more intricate lie perhaps? Or maybe tell the truth.

And what Harry then said – considering this little fishing port, and what they had been talking about before – made perfect sense.

15.

A CONFESSION

KAT WATCHED AS HARRY pointed across the mouth of the river here, the water so flat, calm, the churn of the big boats gone, as if the sea itself here was ready for night, ready to rest.

"See over there, Charlie? Littlehampton Yacht Club. And see that 30-footer, up at the back? Up on the hard?"

Whatever is Harry doing? she wondered.

"That – is my boat."

Really? thought Kat. *My husband has a big sailboat in a yacht club, and I learn of it now?*

Or is this some kind of clever trick?

"Actually," Harry said, then paused. His face again, showing… *something.*

"She's my *father's* boat, but I helped build her. He was good that way. Great sailor, too. Took my mother and me out all the time. Right out there, where you were probably fishing. Day like this, well, is there anything better?"

"Yacht club," Charlie said dismissively. "Place for toffs."

"Oh, you're right, I'm sure. But still, you – doing what you do – must love the sea, the way it changes, the way it never stops. But my sailing days with my father and my mother ended. Lost them both. I was just a boy, really. So, you see, Charlie—"

Kat thinking: *If this was a trick it was a dammed good one…*

"I *know* what it's like to lose a mother, not to have parents. And if I knew what you know about whoever did it? Would I want to kill him?"

Harry let the question hang there.

Then: "Damn right I would."

And somehow, whether it was the fading light, night coming fast, the image of the boat, the way Harry could amazingly connect to this possibly murderous fisherman, Charlie Todd's fists unclenched. He sniffed the air.

Like something slowly breaking, a fortress of sand melting at that first gentle wave that finally reaches it.

He looked at them both, and began.

"ALL RIGHT, I'LL TELL *yers* everything. The truth. First, the hard stuff. So yeah, I did sign up to work in the kitchen for *one* reason. Palmer had ignored me. He didn't care a damn what happened to my poor mother, what he did, her life destroyed. Not me either. Only one thing good enough for that man. Murder."

Kat had a sudden, fearful thought – that maybe Charlie *had* killed Carmody by mistake.

"So, you did it?" she said as gently as she could.

But now slowly, sadly, Charlie shook his head

"No. I planned on doing it. Find a time when the *bastard* was alone, get away without being seen." A sheepish grin then. "Not much of a plan."

"You didn't write a note?"

A head shake. "Note? I didn't write no note. I can hardly write, can I?"

Kat looked at Harry then back to the boy. She knew he was telling the truth.

"Didn't need no note, anyways. All I needed was a minute alone with him."

"So last night – when your work in the kitchen was done – you slipped outside, yes?" said Harry.

"That's right. Out into the woods by the terrace. Waiting. Watching. I reckoned Palmer'd *have* to come outside at some point. Get some air."

"Which he did," said Kat.

"Late it was," said Charlie. "But yeah, he came out. That big mask, like some strange bird. I knew that was him, asked one of the footmen earlier, like."

"Plague Doctor," said Harry.

"I dunno," said Charlie, with a shrug. "Scary thing. Nasty."

"So – he came out – onto the terrace," said Harry.

"Yeah. On his own. Perfect, I thought. So I follows him. Away from the house. Down towards the lake. The grotto. All alone. Me thinking, *this* is it, this is the time."

Kat thought... *all right – going to learn everything now.*

"So when he reaches the grotto, I get my knife out, start to catch up with him, getting ready like. But then *another* bloke comes out of the woods, all creeping low, like he didn't want to be seen."

Kat waited, hardly daring to breathe, to break the moment, as Charlie looked at them both, eyes wide.

"This other bloke, he rushes at Palmer and jumps him and the two of them struggle, then Palmer - least the man I *thought* then was Palmer - falls into the mud, stops moving, the other bloke standing over him, like he wasn't sure what he'd done."

Kat: "Did you see anything else? What the second man wore?"

"Nah, too dark. Big cloak and a mask – that's all I know. But I did see one more thing. The man reached down, ripped the mask off the fellow in the mud. Then – it was like he just stood there, frozen."

"As if something was wrong?" Harry asked.

"Yeah. Like he couldn't believe what he was seeing."

"What happened then?"

"I didn't move, not an inch. Just watched. Didn't understand what was happening. Then I saw the bloke pick up that mask, the plague one – throw it into the lake. And then he was gone. Just disappeared."

"But Charlie," Kat said, having no doubt the man was telling the truth, "didn't you still want to kill Palmer?"

He shook his head. "No. This morning… police involved, you two asking questions? It was suddenly *all wrong*. A real death snapped me out of it." He looked away. "Hate the *bastard*, that's for sure. But I suddenly thought, I'll ruin my life by killing him. That didn't make no sense at all."

And then Kat watched as Harry put a hand on the man's shoulder.

"Charlie, we're damned glad you came to that realisation. If it's any consolation, people like Palmer… well… let's just say they do – sooner or later – get their comeuppance."

Harry's hand remained.

"Think I may get my boat back in the water soon. Been long enough. Going to need some help, you know? The kind of help that someone who works the sea, who knows boats, could provide. So, if you don't mind, when the time comes, I'll look you up."

And then Charlie, who had seemed ready to punch the lights out of both of them and dash away, smiled and said simply, "I'd like that, Sir Harry."

"Grand," said Harry. "Now you'd better get back to your boat. Seems like you have a lot of fish to tend to."

A nod, and Kat watched Charlie turn and walk back along the quay towards the darkening shapes of the fishing boats.

The sky had lost its dazzling colours. A lustrous night was beginning, with a planet in the east suddenly bright. *Jupiter*, Kat thought? No, a red tinge. Appropriately enough. *Mars*. The first bright stars blinking. And even a chilly gust now springing from the sea.

Harry took her arm in his and they walked back along the seafront towards the Alvis, neither of them speaking.

Both of them, she knew, thinking through the implications of what Charlie had told them.

At the car, Harry checked the two crates of fish were secure in the dicky-seat, then they climbed in.

But Harry didn't start the engine.

"You first?" said Harry.

"Was hoping you'd start the theorising."

"Me?" said Harry. "Oh, I'm properly baffled."

Kat laughed. "Okay, let's think about what we know, not what we *don't* know."

"Go ahead."

"Carmody went to the lake wearing Palmer's costume. And whoever killed him was very surprised when they pulled off the mask. They thought they were killing Palmer, not Carmody."

"All of which must make Palmer innocent, right?" said Harry.

"Indeed. It also answers the question of how we saw Palmer playing billiards when Carmody was being killed."

"But Carmody only went down to the lake because somebody invited him to a secret meeting."

"So – a big question," said Kat. "Why did Carmody wear Palmer's mask to the meeting?"

"Yes. Did he choose to? Or was he *made* to?"

"Time to revisit motives, I think," said Harry. "But this time the question being who – besides Charlie Todd – wanted Cyril Palmer dead?"

"A good topic for our drive home."

"Exactly," said Harry, turning to her, "And if we get going, we might just be in time for dinner."

"These crazy roads of yours safe at night?"

And as Harry started up the Alvis, he laughed, saying: "Why, they're even more fun!"

DURING THE HARROWING – to Kat, at least – road trip back at night, she and Harry reviewed what they now knew.

"All right then, what's the plan when we get back? After we've eaten, of course."

"Well, I was rather hoping you'd have some bright ideas in *that* department. You know, American innovation and all."

She laughed. "I guess a few times, back in Manhattan, the truth being elusive, I did see how my boss played it."

"And how's that exactly?"

"He told me later. *Use what you* know *to force out what you don't.*"

"There we are! Couldn't be easier."

They both laughed at that, as Kat could see the same spot on the Downs they had passed hours earlier, now dotted with the barely visible lights from farmhouses, and in the distance the glow of the tiniest of villages.

Looking so beautiful.

"I have another thought," Harry said. "I mean, if we get the chance."

"Yes?"

"Be good to look in Palmer's room. According to Forsyth, Carmody had incriminating papers to hand over. But I didn't find them in Carmody's case. Is that because Palmer stole the papers?"

"You think they might point to the killer?"

"Possible. Right now, I can't see any other way forward. Anyway, we'll soon be back at Mydworth Manor. This is shaping up to be one of our more *interesting* investigations, isn't it?"

To which Kat said in earnest: "Interesting? Frustrating."

But when Harry went up the long drive to the manor house, gravel crunching, the house all aglow, and shedding enough light out front, Kat could see a familiar car parked by the fountain, and someone by it, standing, waiting.

16.

THE MASK DROPS

AS HARRY PULLED the Alvis tight around the circle, just to the front door, Kat saw the old doctor, no bag this time, but simply standing there. And even in the dim light, a worried perplexed expression was visible on his face.

"The good doctor," Harry said.

"And I think," Kat said, "waiting for us."

They hopped out of the car and walked over to him.

"Sir Harry, Lady Mortimer – so very glad you're back. You see, um, I'm not sure how to begin."

The doctor was apparently quite excited, flustered even.

She saw Harry put one hand gently on the doctor's arm, keeping his voice low. Having that calming effect that it always seemed to possess.

She did love that voice.

"Dr Bedell, steady now. You've been waiting for us?"

The doctor nodded. "Yes, everyone's inside, at dinner. But I wanted to catch you straight away."

Harry looked at Kat, half his face catching the light, the other in shadow.

"I see. So, did you find something? About Carmody?"

"Yes. And it's not good, not good at all."

For a man so rattled, it occurred to Kat he was taking his own good time to get the information *out*.

"Those small marks, on the neck? From a syringe! And the autopsy shows something had been injected into poor Mr Carmody."

Kat took a step closer. With the sun down, a chill in the air, bit of a breeze.

"Do you know what was injected?"

"No. That will take a while, to be looked at by the lab. But it seems pretty clear."

"It does?" said Harry.

Bedell nodded. "Oh yes. Whatever it was, triggered a heart attack, or at least what would *look* like a heart attack."

Kat again looked at Harry – and he too had his eyes on her.

"Dr Bedell. Thank you for this. Very helpful. I think for now, we'll take it from here."

"You'll call Sergeant Timms?"

Kat knew what Harry's answer to that would be.

"Shortly, yes. Just need to sort one or two things first."

Bedell nodded as if the suggestion of delaying police involvement made perfect sense.

"Thanks again, doctor."

Bedell – face grim – took his dismissal, after delivering what Kat could only think of as a *bombshell*.

"Well, well, well," said Harry as Bedell went to his car, started it and pulled away. "A syringe."

"Are you thinking what I'm thinking?" said Kat.

"Only one person likely to possess a syringe – Sawyer."

"No difficulty finding a motive there, your honour."

"Jealousy. Oldest one in the book."

"Doesn't necessarily make him the killer though."

"No," said Harry. "Nor does it explain that damned note."

Kat looked across at the house, the ground-floor windows all lit, a gentle hubbub of conversation drifting outside from the dining room.

Then a thought…

"Show me the note again, Harry," she said.

Harry dipped his hand into his jacket pocket, pulled out the envelope, removed the note and gave it to her.

Kat read the simple message.

"Okay. And the envelope?" she said and Harry passed it over.

She looked at the letter, then at the envelope: the simple words "Wilfred Carmody Esq" written on the front. Then she looked back at the letter.

"I've been an idiot, Harry," she said. "The answer was here all along."

"What do you mean?" said Harry moving closer.

"Look at the paper. Then the envelope. I mean… *really* look at it. Feel it."

She waited while Harry examined them both, carefully.

"Dammit," he said. "They *don't* match. Might look the same – but they're different kinds of paper entirely."

"Not just that. Look at the handwriting. It doesn't match either. It's a good attempt – but an amateur one."

"Whoever wrote that letter – didn't write the name on the envelope."

"Exactly," said Kat. "Now I'm only guessing – but my hunch is – Palmer wrote the name 'Wilfred Carmody' on the envelope."

"So *he* got the invite – knew there was something dodgy afoot – and, no pun intended – palmed it off on Carmody."

"You got it."

"I think I'm beginning to see the light," said Harry.

MURDER WORE A MASK

"Me too. There's a bit of work to do, but if we're quick—"

"We can catch ourselves a killer."

"Let's do what we can while people are still at dinner," said Kat. "Can't postpone the local police forever."

"That we can't. But first…"

And Harry turned from Kat, and looked towards the distant greenhouse. "Need to make a quick dash over to Grayer. Get him to round up a couple of footmen and take the rowing boat out onto the lake. See what he can dredge up."

"Good idea."

"Meanwhile, yes, we need to take a look around a few guest rooms before dinner ends."

"I know," said Kat. "I'll go check the Sawyers' room, you check Palmer's."

"And let's hope that no one skips the last course, eh? Meet you in the hall in five?"

And before they went up the steps, Kat touched his arm.

"Harry – we'd better be careful. We *know* it's murder now. And the murderer is here in this house."

And she followed Harry up the stone steps, opening the heavy wooden door.

17.

A GATHERING OF LIARS

HARRY HAD OPENED EVERY drawer of the dresser in Palmer's room, revealing an array of clothes for a gentleman's weekend in the country.

No sign of papers. It was clear there was only one place left to look.

Palmer's briefcase.

Sadly locked, Harry could see, leather flap clicked into place, combination tumblers below.

Of course he could go downstairs, get a knife or scissors to open it.

But, tick-tock he thought. *No time for any of that.*

He went into the en-suite bathroom.

Thinking – there must be *something* of use here.

THE SAWYERS' ROOM LOOKED in complete disarray. A bottle of whisky on a table by the window, clothes carelessly tossed onto a satiny love seat, trunks and cases spilling over.

Looked to Kat like changing for dinner must have gotten a little bumpy and, despite Lavinia having a full staff, there'd been no time yet for any of the maids to tidy up.

All of which made what Kat had to do even more difficult.

Digging through the clothes, patting down the rumpled bed, opening dresser drawers... looking for what?

Where exactly does someone who uses a syringe to take drugs hide such an item?

Would he keep it on his person? Not helpful if that was true.

But then, when she opened the bottom drawer of the claw-footed dresser, topped with a rather baroque and gilded mirror, she saw a silken scarf. And it was wrapped tightly around something *hard*.

Aware that she was moving fast, getting excited, she forced herself to slow down.

This might be it, she reminded herself.

And as she unwrapped, she saw a purple velvet box, held tight with a latch.

She opened the latch to see - the different elements of a syringe. A pair of them, it looked like, nestled sweetly in the recesses of the plush box. No sign of whatever was injected. Kat guessed that would be hidden elsewhere.

No time to find that. But she might just be able to unearth a sample of Sawyer's writing.

She went over to a small bureau that stood open beneath the windows. Various papers were strewn across the surface.

All she needed was something signed by Sawyer himself.

If Harry got lucky too, this was all beginning to piece together...

Between them, were they going to unmask the murderer tonight?

IN PALMER'S BATHROOM, Harry looked at a drawer under the black marble sink.

To see a variety of quite useful items: sticky plasters, ointments, roll of white tape and gauze. All you might need in case of a shaving accident or a nasty tumble on a country ramble.

But then – aha – *scissors*!

He grabbed them and – *everything be damned* – began what turned out to be the difficult task of cutting through the leather clasp of the briefcase.

Thinking: *I have certainly gone over our five-minute deadline.*

He used all the force he could to cut through the last bit of tough leather.

He even grinned when he remembered that brilliant movie with Charlie Chaplin, preparing to feast on, yes, *boiled shoe leather*. Pretty tough indeed!

It tore open, and Harry could pull the case wide and look inside. To see…

Oh yes. These were the papers that Carmody must have had in his room.

A quick rifle through them. Memos about land deals. Formal letters documenting what – at first glance – looked like a slimy *tit for tat* arrangement. Votes being sold, and from the thickness of the stack, years and years of corrupt, though clearly lucrative, dealings.

But most important – the correspondence from Charlie Todd and the sworn affidavits from women who had worked alongside Charlie's mother.

Clear – and damning – proof that Palmer was Charlie's father.

And finally, signed letters from Palmer that – with Kat's trained eyes – would reveal whether or not he had re-addressed the fatal invitation to that meeting at the grotto.

But, no time now for a thorough examination, as Harry, keeping the papers in hand, turned and dashed down to meet Kat.

"SUCCESS?" KAT SAID, seeing Harry holding the papers.

"Absolutely. Papers – the lot. And you?"

"Oh yes. Found syringes, all right. And a very interesting sample of our swashbuckling friend's handwriting."

Harry nodded. "Think we're ready for this?"

"You mean our test of the theory of using what we know to find out what we *don't*?"

"Yes. Or as one might say, let's go shake that tree and see what falls out."

"Put like that, it sounds like a lot of fun."

And she took his hand, and they walked towards the dining room, just like a couple arriving a tad late for dinner.

EVERYONE AT THE GRAND table took notice of them. Though some – now fortified with dessert wines and such – took a bit longer in the chain reaction of taking them in.

Added to the startling effect, Harry thought, was the fact that they were obviously *not* dressed for dinner.

He looked at Kat, and tried to not let his face show that he wasn't at all sure about what they were about to do.

"Um. Excuse me everyone. Dreadfully sorry! We hate to be disturbing puddings and all that. But you see we have something rather urgent to discuss with *all* of you."

Some of the people at the great dinner table had absolutely nothing to do with the events to be discussed, Harry knew. Still, best to get the lot all together. And, either way, they should enjoy the show!

"Lady Mortimer and I, you see, have some rather important things to discuss."

Then Kat offered an edit. "Questions to be asked."

Ah yes, he thought. *Questions. Stoke those fires a bit. No one likes questions.*

He could see, at the head of the table, his aunt, looking smashing of course. And wearing what appeared to be, well, a surprised smile.

Say this for Lavinia, she's always had rather broad taste in what qualifies as after-dinner entertainment.

Let's hope that includes tonight's performance.

People at the table began turning to each other; some looking intrigued, others not terribly pleased, muttering.

So, Harry raised his voice.

"So now, if you will, *everyone*! To the ballroom, please. Should take but a few minutes. Best without the distraction of McLeod's delicious puddings."

He turned to Kat. "Isn't that right, Lady Mortimer?"

Kat nodded, clearly doing her very best to hide her own grin. This was a serious business, but that didn't take away any of the element of thrills and surprise from it, he guessed.

People – a handful of them grumbling – got up from the table.

Palmer shaking his head, doing his best irritated act. No sign there of any alarm. Celine and Douglas Sawyer, slowly getting up, Sawyer shrugging as he tossed down his napkin upon his half-consumed crème brûlée.

Must hunt one of those down later, Harry thought. McLeod wielded the blow torch like a *master*.

Forsyth and Quiller both wore wary looks as they stood up, turning to some of Lavinia's other guests, doing their best pretence of acting clueless.

What in the world is going on?

Then, to bring up the rear, Harry turned to Kat.

"You go first, hmm?"

"Glad to."

Lavinia had hurried back to him as the dining room emptied. "I do hope this little dramatic turn of yours has a point to it?"

Kat answered: "Oh, that it does, Aunt Lavinia. *Exactly* what… well, we don't know *all* that yet."

"But soon to be revealed?"

"That's the idea," said Harry.

"Well, good. After last night's high jinks, this evening's little gathering was certainly in need of something to jazz it up."

"Glad we could help," Harry said, grinning, as the trio turned and walked towards the ballroom.

It is, Harry thought, *showtime.*

Here's hoping we have the right script.

KAT HEARD HARRY clear his throat, silencing the muttering, as he turned to her.

And she started with a bit of surprise. "Mr Benton, please see that anyone who'd like a brandy *has* one? Not sure, despite Sir Harry's promises, how long this will take."

Benton nodded, and departed to organise trays of snifters.

"Now then," Kat started, realising, while she may have attended similar scenes in that lawyer's office back on Park Avenue, taking notes, it was not exactly the same as leading one! "Imagine you are all very curious. All this… drama. But, you see, Sir Harry and I are afraid it's not simply 'drama' that's going on here."

She paused.

Ah to be an actress, she thought.

"It's more of a report," she said, slowly, "about murder."

At that, the room seemed collectively to take a breath.

Kat looked around, the faces now stilled by that terrible word.

"And – worst news – it turns out that the murderer is in this very room."

The assemblage took their cue to fire out an assortment of "whats?" and "my Gods".

Which Kat allowed to subside. If this played out right, she realised, they would soon stop their display of consternation and turn back to take in the main event.

Where more surprises were promised.

18

FUN IN THE BALLROOM

KAT LOOKED AROUND the ballroom, one of the grand rooms in Mydworth Manor that Lavinia so rarely allowed to be opened.

Yards of precious red satin formed perfectly shaped curtains for the ten-foot-tall windows, and the walls were dotted with historical paintings, one or two of them, she knew, by the Old Masters.

One wall was dominated by a giant tapestry of what looked like a rather vigorous fox hunt, with the snarling foxes not cooperating.

And on the far wall – on either side of a gathering of ancient family portraits – hung a bold cluster of lances, pikes and swords, gathered together as one might have placed a faux elephant foot by the front door, filled with umbrellas, should they be needed.

The crowd standing in the room's centre, looking almost as if they might be awaiting a last-minute train announcement, gazed expectantly in the direction of Harry and Kat.

And Harry, with a broad grin, wasted no time.

"JOLLY GOOD. NOW, Lady Mortimer and I are deeply sorry to have interrupted pudding et cetera – it's just that a deuced important thing has popped up."

The sea of people standing in the room were curious, to be sure, but not at all happy with this little show so far.

Hang on, Kat thought. *It's about to get better.*

"You see, dear friends, Kat and I have been doing a little digging around to see, well, whatever there *was* to be seen regarding the good Mr Carmody's untimely passing."

That – at least – prodded Sawyer, his snifter held like a petite chalice at his waist. "*Untimely*? The old sod had a heart attack."

Sawyer, swaying slightly, looked around at the guests, waiting for the nods of agreement which did in fact come.

Kat could see the newspaper magnate Forsyth with his writer Quiller. No nods there, and their eyes showing an intense gleam of interest.

"Well, yes, Sawyer. Did appear that way, old boy, to be sure. But, well… best I let my wife explain it all. She's uncannily good at connecting dots, crossing 'ts' and – in my experience – making the truth clear as glass."

Harry turned to her and Kat gave the slightest roll of her eyes. *Her Harry was… what was the word? A card.*

"THANK YOU, HARRY. So, as my husband has suggested, we now know that Mr Carmody was in fact—" dramatic pause here, "murdered."

Kat waited until the grumbling and muttering ended.

"Good Lord," said Palmer.

"Hard to believe, isn't it, Mr Palmer?" she continued. "But, you see, on the way back here tonight, we ran into Dr Bedell. He had some very interesting news from his colleagues at the morgue in Chichester."

Another pause.

"Turns out that Wilfred Carmody had some unusual pin-point injections in his neck. The work of a syringe, apparently. And worse, I'm afraid, something had been injected into 'old Carmody' as you call him, with the intention of *killing* him. Murder. Clear as day."

Palmer now knew that he had become part of this show, as Kat saw people turning and looking for the man's next riposte.

"Why would anyone want to murder Carmody?" he said. "What in heaven's name would be the motive?"

At that, Kat saw that Forsyth and Quiller, who certainly had opinions on that subject, now actually wore small smiles. Were they perhaps imagining all this playing out on the front pages of their newspaper?

Oh, the sales when those papers hit the streets.

"Motive? Great question. Well, I'll be honest with you, Mr Palmer, at first we did have a bit of a tricky time with that. Sir Harry – best you carry on from here?"

"Absolutely, Lady Mortimer. You see, Mr Carmody was a man of unimpeachable integrity. An honourable man. He went down to the lake last night, because he had received an invitation to do so, apparently from a 'concerned' friend."

Harry stopped, looked around at the faces. Taking his time.

"An invitation to a meeting, that led to his death. Now, as Lady Mortimer and I have investigated this terrible event, it has become clear to us that only one person in this house would benefit from his demise. Only one person had a powerful enough motive to *murder* Wilfred Carmody."

Kat saw Harry pause again, like a seasoned prosecution lawyer, then swivel to face the jury. "Cyril Palmer!"

A wave of "ohs" and "ahs" and mutterings rippled across the room.

But Harry silenced them by raising in the air the stack of paper he had been carrying in his hand, almost triumphant – "Indeed! I found these papers, incriminating papers, in your room, Palmer. Had to ruin your briefcase, old man. Sorry about that. Locked and all."

Palmer's face turned puce, as he practically spat out the next words.

"What the—? I will *sue* you, Mortimer!"

"Imagine you will, old chap," Harry said. "But that's why God created solicitors, no? So, sue away. Anyway, where was I?"

Another grin from him, and Kat thought, *I, too, could not be having a better time.*

Even though a successful end to this performance was – still – far from certain.

"Oh yes, of course. These *papers*. Well, we know – thanks to two talkative little 'birds' – that Carmody was planning on sharing the damning evidence in these papers with the wider world. Isn't that right, Mr Forsyth?"

Forsyth made the slightest of nods.

Harry went on. "I mean, Palmer, you really have done some quite terrible things. Things that, well, might even destroy you. Now, naturally, that seemed like motive enough to us, wouldn't you all agree?"

Kat had her eyes locked on Palmer – knowing they did not have proof of the whole story here.

And that fear deepened when Palmer himself smiled back, took a step forward as if it was his time to shine in the spotlight.

"Oh, *really*… I hate to spoil all this ridiculous 'sleuthing'. But as a number of guests here can verify, I was in the house for the whole damn *time* of whatever transpired down at the grotto."

Kat knew that Palmer's defence wasn't relevant, but letting it play out was certainly amusing.

"The entire time – and then some. Winning a tidy sum at billiards, don't you know. So whatever nonsense you hold in those papers in your fist, Sir Harry – which you *will* pay a legal price for – I could not have done a damned thing."

Kat smiled. As for Harry, she knew he wasn't at all intimidated by Palmer's threats. Even though her husband had sawn though a locked briefcase!

"Well, Palmer, your day in court will come. And I imagine you may have a lot of them 'to come' if even *half* of the revelations in these papers are true. As to—"

Then Kat heard the front door open. The sound of feet.

And a sight that, well, probably didn't occur often, if ever.

Grayer the gardener, big rubber boots on, still wet and muddy, tromping into the ballroom.

And he, too, held something in his hand. Something mucky, dripping lake water.

HARRY WATCHED AS Grayer came up to him. He kept his voice low, clearly aware that whatever he had walked into, all eyes were now on him.

"Sir Harry, found this. Just as you said."

And without ceremony, Grayer handed over the item which in its current muddy, weed-strewn state didn't look like anything much.

To preserve decorum – and all that rigmarole – Harry said: "Thank you Mr Grayer. Lady Mortimer and I will handle this from here on."

And Grayer – dismissed – turned and walked out of the room, creating a new set of muddy tracks on the polished wood floor.

"Now then," Harry said, "here's where all this gets *very* interesting, if it wasn't already. You see, Palmer, yes, of course, we knew you couldn't have been down there, by the grotto. Could not have killed Carmody."

"Then why the hell have you just accused me here in public, you damned—"

"But hang on. Show's not over yet. See, we *do* know that you certainly wanted him dead."

"Nonsense!"

"In fact, we have a witness, whose account of what he saw last night, led us to this," Harry hefted the sodden, dripping item, "which Grayer found just now in the lake. By said grotto. And guess what it is, boys and girls?"

And Harry, seeing Kat watch as if he was a magician about to pluck the biggest rabbit of all time out of a hat, let the crumpled item *unfold*.

To reveal a mask.

And not just any mask, Harry knew.

"I do believe, Palmer, this is *yours*, no? The Plague Doctor mask, which – amazingly – Carmody was wearing last night at the grotto. You see, whoever killed Carmody, thought they were killing *you*. Which leaves one last question. Lady Mortimer?"

The room was still – even Palmer had a sick expression on his face.

Kat spoke. "Yes. Who on *earth* could that have been?"

19.

ONE LAST POINT

KAT SCANNED THE GUESTS. Harry had his eyes on her so she knew it was time for her to wrap up this show. Harry had walked over to Benton.

She guessed he was making a quiet request for the butler to summon Sergeant Timms.

But first...

Kat began. "So now we ask not who wanted to kill *Wilfred Carmody*, oh no. We ask who would want to murder *Cyril Palmer*, esteemed Member of Parliament for these parts? Well, maybe a lot of people wished him ill. But to kill him? With a syringe? Using some deadly substance?"

And Kat swore she felt a chill fill the room, the windows open to the night air. Late summer all right, but in here, suddenly like an electric refrigerator.

"Well, I guess we know who that would be, isn't that right... Douglas Sawyer?"

Another gasp from the room. And Kat noticed those guests near Sawyer – including his wife – step back from him, as if his guilt was somehow contagious.

"And motive? Oh, maybe the most ancient of motives. Your dear wife, Celine and our trusted MP, their little trysts for the last year hardly a state secret. *Jealousy*, Mr Sawyer. Such a dark, suffocating feeling, isn't it?"

"Ridiculous!" said Sawyer, his voice quavering, the unfortunate squeak so evident in this silent, echoing room.

"Oh, and let's not forget," Kat continued, "besides motive, there must be 'means' to think about. In this case, as we now know – a syringe."

Slowly she held up the small velvet case and opened it so all could see.

"Found this in your room, Mr Sawyer," said Kat.

Now all eyes were on the movie star.

He stood silent as if there was not a possible word he could say.

"And that note I mentioned, written to Mr Carmody, inviting him to meet at the grotto? It's in your handwriting. You wrote that note, didn't you? And placed it in Mr Palmer's room?"

"This is all nonsense," said Sawyer. "A tissue of lies. I shall also sue, sue both of you."

"But I guess you didn't figure your unfaithful wife would be so concerned that she'd *warn* Palmer," said Kat. "Who then redirected the note to Mr Carmody and persuaded him to wear the mask. So you ended up killing the very person Palmer needed out of the way."

Now the small crowd turned to look at Palmer, this whole scene playing out as if on a West End stage.

"And Palmer?" said Kat. "For a while there it must have seemed that all the cards were falling your way, hmm?"

For once, Palmer was silent.

Gotcha, thought Kat. Then she turned back to Sawyer. "Terribly ironic, isn't it, Mr Sawyer? You'll hang – all for doing Palmer's dirty work for him."

And at that, with everyone's eyes trained on him, Sawyer moved.

"You can all… go to hell!"

And he pushed through the crowd, and dashed to the clustered weapons on the far wall, reached up, and to the whole room's clear astonishment…

Drew a sword – some kind of heavy cutlass.

"I'm leaving here, and not one of you will stop me!" he squeaked, slicing the lethal-looking weapon through the air above his head.

Kat watched as the actor raced back across the room, the crowd scattering, men and women screaming.

Which is when she saw Harry take a quick run at the other stand of weapons, withdraw a matching sabre, and call out: "Not too sure about that, Sawyer, old chap."

Sawyer stopped dead in his tracks, then laughed.

"You fool, Mortimer – have you seen none of my films? I bloody well know how to use this!"

But Harry just smiled. Then – and was he just being dramatic? – he bowed elegantly and took up a fighting stance, one arm behind his back, his sabre outstretched: "*En garde!*"

And while guests ran around trying to take in the show but avoid becoming another unfortunate victim of any errant thrusts, her husband and Sawyer duelled.

AT FIRST, SAWYER seemed to be getting the best of Harry, and Kat suddenly became worried.

What had been fun, had now turned dangerous.

The blades crashing into each other, both looking as sharp as scythes, the metal edges slicing through the air. Of course, Kat thought, Sawyer had appeared in all those swashbuckling movies. He really knew what he was doing.

And even as Harry took great steps forward, accompanied by forceful thrusts, Sawyer easily swatted them away, his own thrusts and cuts coming within inches of Harry's face.

Each alarming slice summoning a sick groan from the now-frightened crowd.

But even when that occurred, Harry managed to call out, over the clash of metal as he parried, "Don't worry, Kat. Bit rusty, it appears. But I was rather proficient at this back at school. Got a trophy or two around here *somewhere*."

Then Sawyer – in what seemed an impossible move for someone who indulged in intoxicants as much as he did – *leapt* onto one of the banqueting tables, giving him the advantage of height over Harry, who now was mostly ducking and swerving.

Until: "All right, enough of this," Harry said, holding his position, as if to make himself a target.

And when Sawyer then took aim with a great stomach-churning slice - Harry simply *stepped aside*.

Sawyer, off-balance, teetered at the table's edge as Harry's own sabre now shot up, catching the hilt of Sawyer's sword and simply flipping it away into the air.

That movement, adding just enough *push* that Sawyer fell to the floor, landing hard.

Where Harry placed the tip of his sword at the base of the prone man's skull.

"Not bad, Sawyer. But fancy moves? All that cinema stuff? Not terribly useful in a real duel."

Then – incongruously – a bell from outside.

Sawyer moved his arms as if about to get up.

"Oh, please don't," Harry said. "Just a few minutes more."

The bell of the police car – for Kat knew that's what it was – stopped. And, in moments, Sergeant Timms walked into the ballroom.

Cleared his throat.

And said: "Now, um – will someone please explain to me what in Heaven's name is going on here!"

20.

TEA FOR THREE

KAT TOOK A SIP of the tea, exactly as she liked it with two sugars and a squeeze of lemon.

Just a day after the weekend party that had delivered so much more entertainment than Lavinia could possibly have hoped for, Kat and Harry were back at the manor for tea and – to be sure – questions.

Harry's face was catching the sun, though the smell of fall was already in the air.

"I say, Lavinia," said Harry, "has this weekend at all put you off big parties?"

"Oh, I don't know, Harry. You can't say – murder notwithstanding – it all wasn't rather thrilling. I still," she turned and looked at Kat, "do have a few questions, though."

Kat smiled. "Ask away. Not sure we even now understand everything."

"Good then. So – to the rest of the story? How did Palmer set up Carmody to be killed?"

Kat nodded. "We think he suggested that – for fun – they swap masks, in the spirit of the party and all that."

"Ah, I see. And he just slipped the invitation into a new envelope?"

Harry leaned forward. "That's the brilliance of it, Aunt Lavinia. Palmer used a death threat against *himself* to bump off a chap who was about to ruin him. Dashed clever. Nearly got away with it. Would have too – if he'd managed to remove the invitation from Carmody's room before I got there."

"I see," Lavinia said. She took a bite of cookie. "I *think*. But will Palmer go to jail?"

Kat looked to Harry for that one.

"Ah, good question. Passing the note, swapping the mask, all that. One could make a case that he was a conspirator in murder. But I suspect a good solicitor will get him off."

"I do hope not," Lavinia said.

"Either way, he will be ruined, in disgrace. No worries about that."

"And Celine? I mean, we go back such a long way. And such a lovely voice."

Kat reached out and touched Lavinia's hand. The more she spent time with Harry's aunt, the more she liked her.

"She will be in trouble, since she must at some point have figured out what was happening and then kept quiet. But her only overt action if you will, was warning Palmer. Think at the very least, she may want to go abroad for some time. That is, if she is not charged."

"Maybe Australia? One hears so many people do that these days. Me, I couldn't ever. I mean, those kangaroos? What on earth kind of animal is that?"

Kat laughed.

But then Lavinia tilted her head.

"One more question. Then we can just enjoy the sun and talk about... I don't know, the latest book you've read?"

"Fire away," Harry said.

"Bravo you two… but now what? No projects at the Dower House? Whatever will you do?"

"Always things needed at the Woman's Voluntary Service," Kat said. "Nicola's doing amazing work for the women of the area."

Lavinia smiled as if she had a secret. "She is incredible. But is that *enough*, after all—?"

And Harry stood up as if looking into the distance.

"Well you see, Lavinia, you know we went to Littlehampton—"

"Indeed," said Lavinia. "The fish were delicious. I've had McLeod put in a regular order."

"Jolly good," said Harry. "Anyway, while we were there, I saw the old boat."

"Your father's yacht. Yes. She was a beauty."

Harry nodded. "Been in drydock a long time, but the yard has looked after her pretty well. And I'm thinking, well wouldn't that be a great project for Kat and me? Get her fixed up, take her out to sea before the autumn sets in. Maybe you could join us on board for a sundowner one evening?"

Kat saw Lavinia hesitate as if thinking the proposition over, or perhaps thinking about other things. But then – the warmest of smiles.

"Now that's a splendid idea. Just like the old days. I'll even help."

"Good!" Harry said. "Now where's the champagne when you need it? I should summon Benton."

But Kat looked at her husband, and said: "Harry – Sir Harry – I think tea is just fine for now."

And he nodded back at her, sat down, with Kat thinking, *Wherever will that sailboat take us?*

Time will tell.

NEXT IN THE SERIES:

DEADLY CARGO

MYDWORTH MYSTERIES

Matthew Costello & Neil Richards

Mydworth's Excelsior Radio Company is world-famous for its expensive radio-phonographs. But suddenly the Excelsior delivery lorries start being hijacked, and the very future of the company is in doubt. Can it just be about the stolen radios – or is there something more secret and dangerous going on?

When Harry and Kat are brought in to help, they decide to go undercover to solve the crimes and soon discover there are many more secrets to this mystery than meets the eye…

ABOUT THE AUTHORS

Co-authors Neil Richards (based in the UK) and Matthew Costello (based in the US), have been writing together since the mid-90s, creating innovative television, games and best-selling books. Together, they have worked on major projects for the BBC, PBS, Disney Channel, Sony, ABC, Eidos, and Nintendo to name but a few.

Their transatlantic collaboration led to the globally best-selling mystery series, *Cherringham*, which has also been a top-seller as audiobooks read by Neil Dudgeon.

Mydworth Mysteries is their brand new series, set in 1929 Sussex, England, which takes readers back to a world where solving crimes was more difficult — but also sometimes a lot more fun.

MURDER WORE A MASK